The Adventure:

FROGGER

Frank B. Edwards

To Nicola

[signature]

Illustrated by John Bianchi

🌿Pokeweed Press

Written by Frank B. Edwards
Illustrated by John Bianchi
Edited by Susan Dickinson
Copyright 2000 by Pokeweed Press

Third printing 2006

Cataloguing in Publication Data

Edwards, Frank B., 1952-
  Frogger

(Adventures of Bug and Frogger)

ISBN 1-894323-19-X (pbk.)   ISBN 1-894323-20-3 (bound)

I. Bianchi, John II. Title. III. Series: Edwards, Frank B. 1952-
Adventures of Bug and Frogger

PS8559.D84F76 2000   jC813'.54   C00-900225-1
Pz7.E2535Fr 2000

Published by:
Pokeweed Press, Suite 337
829 Norwest Road
Kingston, Ontario
K7P 2N3

Printed in Canada by:
Friesens Corporation

Visit Pokeweed Press on the Net at:
www.Pokeweed.com

Send E-mail to Pokeweed Press at:
mail@Pokeweed.com

Contents

The characters in this book are the sort of people that the author has known all his life. But everyone in Tichburg is fictional, so we apologize to those who think they may recognize themselves.

Getting Ready for Work

At exactly 7 o'clock on Friday morning, August 27, Thaddeus Archibald — better known as Frogger to his family and friends — woke up to the irritating buzz of his alarm clock. He slapped sleepily at the snooze button until the buzzer stopped, then stretched out under his blanket to savor the start of his first day as a full-fledged babysitter. By nightfall, he would be $32.50 richer.

The sun was streaming in through his window, and the birds in the side yard were chirping spiritedly over ownership of a large worm. Peanut, his guinea pig, squeaked loudly back at them. Downstairs, he could hear his parents already at the kitchen table, the clink of cutlery on china indicating that breakfast was under way.

Deciding that he could afford five more minutes in bed, he tucked his arms under his head and went over his financial calculations one more time. At 6½ hours a day, charging $5 an hour, he would earn $162.50 a week babysitting the Terrible Troth Twins. Even though the summer holidays were almost over, he would easily make enough money to pay for a pair of RetroTred Hoopster basketball shoes in time for his tryout with the local midget basketball team.

When the alarm clock buzzed again, Frogger rolled out of bed, slapped the OFF button twice and headed downstairs for a quick, almost totally nonnutritious breakfast. He just knew that this was going to be a perfect day.

* * *

His parents were at the kitchen table. His mother sat munching whole-wheat toast and sipping coffee to the sound of the early-morning news, while Frogger's father rummaged through his briefcase, pulling out yesterday's leftovers — newspapers and bits of sandwich and fruit — to make room for the new day's essentials. As usual, he was letting nothing go to waste — not even his garbage — directing banana peels and apple cores into the compost bucket and scanning the old paper for supermarket coupons or juicy news items that might serve as inspiration for his next editorial. Only after he had found five coupons worth a total of $1.79 did he toss the newspaper into the designated recycling bin and stop for a gulp of coffee.

Frogger shook the last handful of Cocoa Buddies into the bowl that his mother had set out for him, splashed some milk over them and headed for the breadbox next to the toaster in search of whatever fruit-filled pastry had survived this late into the week. It was Friday, which meant that there was only one more day to go until the weekly grocery trip. But until then, edible food — his kind of edible food — was in short supply.

There was one cranberry-apple flaky left, and he ate it cold, having decided that the toaster wasn't going to help the taste.

"You should have a glass of milk with that, honey," suggested his mother absentmindedly, well aware that Frogger never drank milk before noon. At breakfast, milk was to be taken only with sugar-saturated cereal on a spoon. Full glasses of milk required peanut-butter sandwiches or chocolate-chip cookies, neither of which would likely be available until at least tomorrow or possibly Sunday. It was odd, thought Frogger, how they never ran out of milk or grain-filled bread.

"Well, boys, it's time for me to go," announced Mrs. Archibald as she slipped a sandwich and a sheaf of papers into her shoulder bag. She was an office manager at the general hospital in town and liked to get to work early.

"Frogger, I don't want you to make any plans for going to the fair until you've cleaned Peanut's cage. Your room is getting messier every week, and a smelly guinea pig cage is more than I can bear. Some days, I wonder how you can live in that room."

"Sure, Mom, I'll do it when I get home."

In his excitement about his babysitting job, Frogger had almost forgotten about the weekend's Harvest Fair. This year, he would even have some serious money to spend.

"And, honey, don't forget to lock the house when you go to the twins'." She blew him a kiss, which he ducked, as she headed out the door.

"Twins?" His father looked up from his coffee, nibbling on the stale remnants of one of yesterday's morning-glory muffins before tossing it reluctantly into the garbage can. "Don't tell me you've got twins, Frogger? Where do you

7

keep them? Not in your room, I hope!"

"The Troth twins," groaned Frogger in exasperation, wondering how much his father had actually heard on Wednesday night when he had agreed that Frogger could take the new babysitting job. "I'm starting work for the Troths today, minding Kenny and Kerry. Remember? Seven-thirty to 2 o'clock . . ."

". . . five days a week and some weekends when school goes back," his father interrupted. "I remember. It's just too early in the day for total recall."

Frowning, Mr. Archibald changed the subject.

"By the way, Mrs. Gilmore dropped off a pager for you late last night. She said you'd know all about it."

He pointed toward a small, bright red ElectroMart bag on the counter beside him, then headed for the sink, a coffee cup in one hand and his briefcase in the other.

"She apologized for the color but said it was the last one in stock. I didn't know what she was talking about, so I just took the bag and told her you would drop by today, after your babysitting job."

Glancing up at the clock, he pulled his car keys from his pocket and was almost out the door before he turned back to say good-bye to Frogger.

"Catch you later, buddy. An 11-year-old with a pager, eh? I think it's time you and I had a man-to-man talk. Maybe you can explain how those things work — after *I'm* through telling you about girls. See you tonight."

And with that, the screen door slammed shut and Frogger was alone, left to take care of himself until at least 6 o'clock.

Tichburg's Lone Wolf

Frogger's mother never left her office before 5:30 in the afternoon, and his father, the editor of the local weekly newspaper, usually stayed until 7:00 on Fridays preparing the Saturday edition for the printer. Both of his parents worked in Wamble, about a 20-minute drive away, but they never seemed to worry about leaving Frogger on his own. Not that anyone was ever really alone in Tichburg.

He had lived here most of his life, and everyone in the village — all 473 people — knew him well. Mrs. Gilmore lived on the corner of their dead-end street and kept a particularly close eye on him — and on everyone else in the neighborhood for that matter. She was the volunteer district fire chief and, in the summer, never strayed far from the big veranda that practically encircled her house. She stayed close to her phone in case a fire call came in, and if she wasn't at home, she was sure to be at the fire station just around the corner.

Because Frogger did a lot of errands for her so that she could monitor emergency calls, Mrs. Gilmore had suggested getting him a pager. Although he wasn't exactly fighting fires, Frogger had become a sort of auxiliary assistant to the fire chief. The job had kept him pretty busy over the summer holidays, which was a good thing, because there wasn't a lot for kids to do in Tichburg.

As an only child, Frogger had learned how to entertain himself early in life, a talent that had become more valuable as he grew older. Kids his age had always been in short supply in Tichburg. His best friend Sean had moved away in grade four, and Casey had left the year after, leaving only four other kids old enough to play with. These days, Kim, Tracy and Janice were too busy dreaming about themselves to pay him any attention, and Roger Grieves was a moron. Out of necessity, Frogger had become a loner — a lone wolf is what Mrs. Gilmore called him. He got along well with everyone but seldom sought out the company of other kids. The fire department and Mrs. Gilmore kept him busy in his spare time, and there was never any shortage of other people to visit or to run errands for.

* * *

He quickly cleared the table, tossing the empty cereal box into a recycling bin, rinsed the dishes in the sink and loaded them into the dishwasher before racing upstairs to his room. He had 15 minutes to get to the twins' house, plenty of time given that they lived just at the end of the street, but he didn't want to be late on his first day. He was their third babysitter that summer, and he needed to keep the job long enough to earn $100 for the new RetroTreds.

The twins would be a challenge — they were 4-year-old terrors with a reputation for getting into everything — but, according to his father, their parents were likely to be the worst part of the job. High-strung and impractical was how his father had described them, claiming that their arrival in Tichburg was a sign — a bad sign — of things to come if every old house in the village was going to be snapped up by snooty city people.

Frogger actually knew little about the Troths or their kind except that they had arrived six months ago after having spent a fortune fixing up the old Davis house, which overlooked the river. Usually, he only saw them as they raced down the street and through the village — Mr. Troth alone in his small roadster and Mrs. Troth in the monstrous red Lincoln Navigator truck that Mrs. Gilmore had nicknamed the Red Menace. The Troths always seemed to be in a hurry.

Dunston Troth was a real estate agent, and his wife Sara was an antique dealer who planned to open a new store in Tichburg once a suitable location became available. For now, they both worked an hour's drive to the east, in Amaranth, the city where they had lived before they moved to Tichburg.

Frogger had met Mr. Troth on Wednesday, when little Kenny had tripped on a crack in the sidewalk out in front of Birdie Pickett's Lucky Dollar store. He was lying there screaming, pounding his pudgy fists and feet into the pavement, while his brother Kerry looked on, gleefully sucking the straw of a juice box.

Because Mr. Troth had seemed so helpless, his arms too full of groceries to do anything but bend down to try to shush the crying boy quiet, Frogger had jumped off his bike and scooped up Kenny, brushing the grit from his skinned knees while the child screamed in his ear. Mr. Troth had stood looking perplexed, fumbling with the keys to the Red Menace, glancing around as if a howling kid were the most embarrassing thing on Earth. But before they could say anything to each other, Frogger had noticed Kerry heading for the street between two parked cars, and with Kenny still wailing in one arm, he had reached out and hauled Kerry back to safety while Mr. Troth balanced his grocery bags precariously against the door of the truck.

"You're very good with children," Mr. Troth had said as he finally dumped the groceries on the seat. "Have you had much experience with youngsters? Preschoolers, I mean."

"I just graduated from a babysitting course," Frogger had explained. "And I plan to be a safety patroller when school goes back next month. I'll be in grade seven." As an afterthought, he had added, "I come from a very safety-conscious family."

And that slim bit of information had been enough for the twins' father. Their latest sitter had just left them with no warning, said Mr. Troth, and the twins were in desperate need of a sitter. Frogger, who had guessed that it was actually Mr. Troth who was most in need, had accepted the job of babysitter to the Terrible Twins on the spot, partly influenced by the promise of $5 an hour — twice his going rate for chores.

That night, while Mrs. Troth was digesting the fact that her husband had hired a complete stranger to care for their precious babies, Frogger had convinced his parents that he was old enough for the job, assuring them that up close, the twins seemed to be much better behaved than their reputations suggested and that the job would enable him to buy a brand-new pair of gel-support high-top basketball shoes — the incredible RetroTred Hoopsters. Besides, he had argued, he had done a better job of helping Kenny than Mr. Troth had — not to mention saving Kerry's life. The twins were probably in better hands with him than they were when out with their father.

And so, this Friday morning saw Frogger quickly preparing for his first official job as a babysitter. After a two-minute grooming session in the bathroom, he assessed the two mounds of clothes on the floor beside his bed, trying to decide which one was clean and which was dirty. Pulling some clothes out of one of the tangled piles, he hurriedly dressed before charging downstairs and out the door, carrying a backpack loaded with an assortment of surefire babysitter aids.

He was halfway across the porch when he realized that he hadn't locked the door. Then, as he was turning his key in the lock, he remembered Mrs. Gilmore's pager. Racing back into the kitchen, he rooted around until he found the ElectroMart bag, slipped it into his pocket and dashed out the door.

First Impressions

Mrs. Troth made no effort to mask her horror when Frogger arrived at her front door at 7:27. His hair was combed, his teeth were brushed, and his shirt and jeans were as clean as they were going to get (for he had chosen the wrong pile of laundry), but the gawking look on Mrs. Troth's face made him wonder whether something was wrong.

Casually checking the fly of his pants with his left hand, he opened the screen door with his right hand. Satisfied that his zipper was as high as it could go, he introduced himself cheerfully.

"Hi, I'm Frogger."

Silence.

"I live just down the street in the little white house . . ."

He paused. Still silence.

"Your husband asked me to babysit for you this week."

"Frogger?" she croaked unsteadily.

14

"Yes, ma'am, it's my nickname. In kindergarten, everyone called me Tadpole because I was small for my age and my real name is Thaddeus, or Tad for short, and . . . ." Realizing she was barely listening, he cut his explanation short. "So when I grew up, people just started to call me Frogger."

"Oh, of course," she replied weakly. Turning, she disappeared deeper into the house, abandoning Frogger at the door as she summoned her husband in an icy-cold tone.

"Dunston. Your young sitter is here . . . ," he heard her call before a slammed door blocked out any further conversation. He didn't appreciate the way she had said "young," the same way someone might say stupid or lazy.

While he waited, unsure of what to do, Frogger peered around, intrigued by the transformation the house had undergone since old Miss Davis had died. Even when she lived there, the place had been falling apart, for its elderly owner had been unwilling to spend the money necessary to fix it up. Frogger, like the other kids in his school, had grown up believing that the big, old brick house at the end of Riverview Road was haunted. The presence of a dozen or more furtive cats had done nothing to change their minds.

But today, he could barely believe his eyes or his nose. The cat smell was completely gone, replaced by the smell of fresh paint and, he thought, money. The house looked like some fashion-magazine mansion. The golden oak staircase and wooden floors had been completely refinished and were gleaming as only old wood can. And the walls, once covered with ancient dark wallpaper, were bone-white and decorated with framed photographs of distinguished-looking people who had probably lived back in the days when this house was new.

Frogger was halfway down the hall closely inspecting the portraits when he heard a door open, followed by the heavy footsteps of Mr. Troth and a snatch of Mrs. Troth's voice, which seemed to be choked with tears.

"So glad you made it, Tad — and right on time. Great. Excellent. Super," he boomed, shaking Frogger's hand as he steered him toward the bottom of the stairs. "Sara and I have to be off to work now, but I will give you a quick tour upstairs. The boys should be asleep for a while longer." He continued in this jolly way for several minutes as he swept Frogger from room to room, showing him bathrooms, bedrooms, a playroom and a second staircase that led back down to the kitchen. Every room was immaculately tidy, toys and clothing neatly stacked and stored as if the house were a department store. Mrs. Troth was in the spotless kitchen silently reapplying her makeup and looked up when they emerged from the narrow back staircase.

"How old are you?" she asked.

"Almost 12, Mrs. Troth, but don't worry, I have plenty of experience babysitting. Haven't lost a little kid yet." His joke had no impact on the twins' mother.

"I'm sure you haven't, but as you can imagine, I am not used to leaving the boys with strangers, and you do seem young."

"Oh, I'm no stranger," ventured Frogger. "We're neighbors actually. I've lived nearly my whole life on this street. You drive past me about 10 times a day."

Mrs. Troth looked as if she was about to say that she had

16

never seen him before in her life when her husband interjected.

"Sara, dear, Frogger . . . I mean, Tad lives in that cute little white house with the huge maple tree in the side yard. The one the Fergusons were admiring when they came for a visit last week . . . ," his voice trailed off as his wife's face brightened.

"Oh, yes, I waved at your mother the other day as I drove by. Yes, we are neighbors, aren't we? Super." And with that, she seemed to accept Frogger as the answer to their childcare dreams. She ushered him to the refrigerator upon which hung six typewritten sheets of instructions for the care and feeding of the twins. She showed him the food they could eat, the food they could not eat, an extra bathroom, a closet filled with outdoor clothes and a locked door that led to the back porch, which overlooked the backyard. Beyond the lawn was the river, Tichburg's most famous feature — loved by kids and feared by mothers for the entire 200 years that the village had been inhabited.

"Of course, we do not let the boys use the backyard. They are not allowed off the back porch unless they are holding our hands. For now, I think you had better keep this door locked," said Mrs. Troth as she headed toward the front hallway with her husband following closely behind. Pausing at the front door, she looked longingly up the stairs.

"The boys should be awake about 8 o'clock. Have fun with them, but try to stick to their schedule. A steady routine is so important. Now, we love this house and ask you to treat it like your own — perhaps even better. Our phone numbers are on the refrigerator, so if you have questions, call us. Good-bye."

And with that, the Troths left. A minute later, Frogger heard the roar of the Red Menace as it headed out the driveway and down the street, followed by the throaty growl of Mr. Troth's roadster.

Frogger was most definitely alone in the old Davis house, which he had once thought was haunted. But ghosts would be the least of his problems on this particular day.

The Terrible Twins

Checking the old pendulum clock above the limestone fireplace that dominated one of the kitchen walls, Frogger calculated that he had about 15 minutes before he would have to deal with the twins — enough time to read the Troths' instruction manual.

Evidently the work of Mrs. Troth (Frogger had seen Mr. Troth in action and knew that he could never have come up with such a list), the six pages of type were divided into three main parts and crammed full of everything a babysitter could do to ruin the lives of kids. Part One covered the twins' care (no television, no running, no climbing) and feeding (no nuts, no sweeteners — artificial or natural — no salt). It was largely line after line of rules, most of which began with the word NO, that eventually gave way to the Troth Twin Mission Statement:

Kenny Troth and Kerry Troth are precious and unique indi-

viduals in this world, with their own special perspectives of the world around them, and have their own roles to play in that world. Their twinness may make them even more special but should never be used as a label of convenience, for each is his own perfect and separate self.

What they really mean, thought Frogger, is that these kids are spoiled — very spoiled — and even though they are twins, they are treated as if they were each an only child. (Not that being an only child was any guarantee of being spoiled. Frogger could testify to that.)

Part Two of the instructions provided a rigid daily timetable of planned activities that seemed to have been conceived to be as boring as possible, and Part Three was a page full of phone numbers and names of people who should be contacted in the event of any imaginable emergency. Scanning the list, Frogger noted that Mrs. Gilmore's number was not included, which made no sense because everyone knew she was the person to call no matter what kind of trouble was brewing.

Certainly on that cold winter night when Birdie Pickett had awakened to the sound of burglars prowling about in her store, she had not called the police because she knew that every lottery ticket and chocolate bar would be stolen before anyone could drive out from Wamble in a patrol car. She had simply called Mrs. Gilmore, who had summoned the entire fire department to the scene of the crime.

Emerging from the door with their booty, the two thieves had found themselves face-to-face with 27 raincoated volunteer firefighters, looking down the wrong end of six fire hoses held by cold, unhappy fellows who would have preferred to be at home in bed asleep. With a roar, Randy Timmerman had turned his hose on the hapless crooks, knocking them off their feet. The remaining hose-wielding firefighters followed suit. The water had frozen on the sidewalk within seconds of leaving the hoses, and the suspects were soon being blasted back and forth across the slippery surface to the hoots and hollers of the firefighters and the handful of neighbors who had arrived to investigate the fuss.

By the time the police arrived, the firefighters had finished playing their game of bad-guy hockey, and the ice-shrouded burglars had been taken over to the fire station to be warmed up, dried off and locked up. They had been handed over to the police wrapped in blankets, shivering with cold and, perhaps, fear. Everyone was home in bed by 3 o'clock — except for Birdie, who was awake all night trying to figure out how she was going to melt the thick crust of ice that covered the windows and door of her store where the water had splashed up off the sidewalk. For the next few days, until the ice had finally melted, customers wanting groceries had to go into her apartment and enter the store through the storage room that led to the video section. It had been a trying experience for Birdie, but her business almost doubled those following days as everyone flocked to the Lucky Dollar to hear her version of the story — and to check out her apartment.

As Frogger was about to examine the breakfast part of the schedule (Balkan yogurt, prune juice, whole-grain toast), he heard a howl and crying coming from the top of the main stairs. Rushing through the kitchen and out into the hallway, he looked up to see the twins, one crying breathlessly while the other stood back smirking. The crier was still in his pajamas; the smirker wore nothing.

"Hi, guys. Remember me?" warbled Frogger in his most cheerful, upbeat voice. "What's the matter with Kenny?"

"I'm Kenny," challenged the naked twin. "That's Kerry, and there's nothing wrong with him."

"Well, there seems to be something wrong," Frogger replied.

"Not really. Kerry just cries whenever we have a babysitter."

"Is that true?" Frogger asked the sobbing child.

"Yes," heaved Kerry through his tears. "I always cry at babysitters. Just for a little while."

"So there's nothing wrong?"

"No."

"Nothing hurts?"

"No."

"You didn't have an accident?"

"I don't drive trucks," Kerry said indignantly.

"I mean, you didn't wet the bed," Frogger explained.

"No."

"But I did," Kenny interrupted. "I always pee for babysitters. Kerry cries. I wet the bed. And my pants."

With that, he started shrieking with laughter, which set Kerry off again. Frogger climbed the stairs, scooped up Kerry and led Kenny to the bathroom. Kerry's tears immediately dried up as he became interested in what was happening. Frogger actually had no idea what he was going to do next. The Troths' instructions, so far as he could recall, did not cover bed-wetting, and it also seemed to have been ignored in his babysitting course. But common sense had led him to

22

the bathroom, where he sat Kerry down atop the counter and assessed the situation.

Kenny had climbed into the old-fashioned cast-iron bathtub and was using the sloping back as a slide.

"Kenny is climbing," tattled Kerry.

"Am not."

"Are too."

"Not."

"Too."

"Well, I won't tell," announced Frogger to settle the argument. "But we do have to get everyone cleaned up for breakfast, so let's run some water in the tub so you can scrub yourselves."

Gingerly, he lifted Kenny from the tub, ran some warm water and, when it was two inches deep, announced that it was ready. Without a moment's hesitation, Kenny leaped in headfirst, sliding down the sloping back and sending a tidal wave of water over everything — including Kerry, who started howling again.

This is going to be a long day, thought Frogger, as he snuggled Kerry into a thick, yellow bath towel and tossed a washcloth and soap into the tub for Kenny.

* * *

By the time the twins were clean, dried and dressed, it was well past 9 o'clock and the perfectly neat bathroom had been reduced to a disaster zone. Sodden piles of towels and clothes were separated by puddles of water that had somehow escaped the tub as the boys slipped and slid from one end to the other — arguing constantly.

No doubt it was the promise of a breakfast of prune juice and whole-grain toast that finally lured the pair out of the bathroom and toward the kitchen, but before Frogger could stop them, they were plunging full speed toward the top of the stairs. A split second before Frogger could grab them, they spun around and threw themselves belly-down onto the floor, just out of reach. Pushing off from the top step, they launched themselves feet-first down the stairs, their little tummies bouncing giddily over all 20 steps, and landed in a squirming, laughing heap at the bottom.

Frogger, relieved that the twins had not killed themselves, sat down on the top step and began slowly bumping down one step at a time.

"This is the way you guys should be going down the stairs," he explained. "The other way is too dangerous."

"It's fun," argued Kerry.

"You do it the baby way," said Kenny.

"Well, I don't think your parents would like your way," countered Frogger, recalling the NO nature of the activity list.

"Nope, don't expect they would," barked a rough voice from the kitchen doorway. "Fella could take a mean tumble down them stairs."

The twins fell silent as Frogger jumped to his feet and peered over the banister. Below him, silhouetted against the kitchen entrance, was a grizzled old man leaning on a cane.

Cigar Davis

"You must be Frogger," the old fellow said as he eased his weight onto his cane and moved forward into the hallway. "And you young 'uns must be twins. By golly, ya look like two peas in a pod."

He shook his head as he looked from one boy to the other, then turned his attention back to Frogger.

"I'm Cigar Davis. Dolly sent me down to see ya. She's been ringing some blasted beeper gadget to get yer attention all morning 'n finally gave up 'n told me to come find ya."

"Who's Dolly?" asked Kenny, who had scampered with Kerry in tow to the safety of the tenth step, where Frogger stood.

"He means Mrs. Gilmore. The lady with the big house on the corner," explained Frogger, as he gathered the twins into his arms.

"That's about the only Dolly in this village I know of, son," laughed Cigar, drawing breath like a wheezy bellows.

"I didn't hear the pager go off."

"That's what she figured. Said ya probably didn't have it on right or somethin'. Me, I don't know the first darn thing about 'em — just seemed easier to walk down than keep dialin' that confounded phone. Too many fool buttons to push ta get anythin' done these days. If ya ask me, t'was better when ya just cranked a phone set. Ya got the operator, told her what ya wanted, bid her a good day, 'n in an hour, everyone knew yer business. Now that was communication."

Frogger was confused but assumed that the old man was not dangerous if Mrs. Gilmore had sent him. "What did she want me for?"

"Wanted to make sure yer wearing that little beeper thing. Hah, she really just wanted me out from underfoot. But she said I could probably get ya to cut my hair — for a small fee, of course."

"Hair? Cutting hair? Your hair?" stammered Frogger. By this time, he had sat back down on the stairs and the old man had rounded the banister and was in full view. He was a big man, somewhat stooped over, but still close to six feet tall. His white hair and beard were long and tangled, giving him the look of Santa Claus at the end of a very long wilderness expedition. He wore a plaid shirt, old green work pants held up by suspenders and a pair of worn corduroy bedroom slippers. A battered straw fedora sat atop his head.

"Mrs. Gilmore said I would cut your hair?"

"Yep. More or less. Sez she's too busy gettin' ready for the Harvest Fair this weekend, bakin' 'n the like. I'm just back from down South, 'n as ya can see, I'm in serious need of a trim."

It was hard to disagree with him, so Frogger just nodded. The twins looked up at him in admiration.

"Ya cut hair, do ya?" asked Cigar.

"Just my dad's. He's going a bit bald, so I just take the electric clippers and give him a buzz cut every two weeks. Anyone could do it."

"Yep, that's what Dolly said," chuckled the old man. "I stopped by yer house to get the clippers. Figured they'd be in the bathroom. 'N there they were. Ya can do it out on the porch, so's we don't mess up this grand house."

"You went into my house and got our clippers from our bathroom?" asked Frogger timidly.

"No problem at all, my boy," Cigar admitted. "T'wasn't locked, 'n I know that house pretty well. Used to live there, ya know. Me 'n the wife moved in when we wuz first married, in 1935. Nice place still. You folks haven't done much to it. Not like this house."

He turned and took in the walls and stairs and glanced back toward the modern kitchen.

"Now these folks, they must have money. More than they know what to do with, looks like. Pretty, though, eh?"

"You remember this house too?" Frogger asked.

"You betcha. Grew up here, didn't I?"

Of course, thought Frogger. This was old Miss Davis's older brother Cyril.

* * *

While the twins settled down to their breakfast of toast and yogurt, Frogger watched Cigar rummage through the kitchen cupboards until he had found coffee beans so that he

27

could "mug up." He explained that two days on a Greyhound bus from Tampa, Florida, without a decent cup of coffee had left him feeling out of sorts and that the sooner he got some good strong coffee in his belly, the sooner his constitution would be back to normal. He had arrived in the town of Wamble at 6 a.m., mooched a ride to Tichburg with Orville Waters, who was just starting his milk run to the area dairy farms, and had made Dolly Gilmore's kitchen his first stop.

"Got on that bus late Tuesday night 'n wuz dreamin' of eggs 'n bacon 'n toast 'n taters 'fore we crossed the Georgia line. The food they expect ya ta eat at those rest stops is bad, but the prices are worse. Mind ya, I knew all that 'fore I even bought my ticket. Friend o' mine gave me a loaf o' squishy white bread 'n a jar o' peanut butter. Ate sandwiches when I wuz hungry 'n dreamed of a big feed the rest o' the time."

The twins sat speechless, yogurt dripping off their spoons and their chins while Cigar described in detail the characters who had accompanied him on his long journey north. If he was to be believed, he had been the only upstanding and completely honest passenger on that Greyhound bus. In his mind, at least, everyone else around him was running or hiding from someone. Their families. Their friends. The police. Most of them had no money; some had dubious plans about how to get rich; and others were hatching plots as they rode north.

"Let's just say, didn't meet a body with steady work or a prayer o' gettin' any," Cigar concluded. "Ya can imagine how happy I am ta be home now, Frogger. I'm gonna get m'self a job 'n a room somewhere. Plenty o' big ol' houses in this

28

village — heck, plenty o' room in this one. Figure someone'll make space fer me."

Frogger assumed that Cigar was at least 85 and truly wondered just what his job prospects might be in a village where everyone seemed to drive into Wamble or the city of Amaranth for work, but he said nothing. The coffee had started flowing through the Troths' shiny black coffee maker but not all of it was ending up in the pot. Cigar jumped up, grabbed a dishcloth from a drawer and mopped up the mess haphazardly. With a final hiccup of steam, the machine finished spitting coffee in and around the pot. Cigar poured himself a cup.

"Where's your wife, mister?" asked Kenny, eyeing his guest warily as the old man sat across from him.

"Gone now. Long gone. Died 15 years ago." He paused. "Wait. You jus' sit tight, 'n I'll fetch a picture of her."

He heaved himself up from the table and headed into the hallway, returning a few seconds later with a heavy framed picture of a young woman who was smiling shyly, her hands carefully folded on her lap, her back straight and her legs barely showing beneath her long skirt.

"That's her. Must'a been all o' 16 then, just 'fore we got married. Don't know how she came to be on the wall in this house, but that's her. Noticed her right off when I came in — just sittin' pretty there, surrounded by strangers. Don't know any of those other folks, though."

He paused for a second, leaned the portrait against the fireplace and reached for his coffee, en route to the refrigerator.

"Dolly's too busy to offer breakfast. Let's see what yer folks've got. Hmmmm. No eggs. No bacon. No taters to fry up.

Prune juice? Yogurt? Hello . . . tofu? No thank ya, boys. Think I'll skip back up to Dolly's once I get m'self that haircut. Maybe if I look a mite sharper, she'll feel more kindly toward me.

"You little 'uns, go fetch me a big tablecloth. 'N a clothespin to fasten it 'round my neck. Frogger, get a kitchen chair 'n a broom. I'll take the clippers out back to the porch."

As he reached for the clippers, Cigar spotted the bright red ElectroMart bag with the pager in it and hauled out the device.

"Ya'd better put 'er on, young fella. Dolly sez she might need ya if there's a fire call. She wants ya to wear it — even if ya don't like the color."

For a moment, Frogger was going to ask why everyone was so concerned about the color. After all, a pager was a pager, and any reasonable auxiliary assistant to the fire chief was unlikely to care about color. But his lofty thoughts were shattered when he actually caught sight of the pager.

It was pink. Bright neon-pink. If Barbie dolls wore pagers, this was the color they would be. Brighter than bubble-gum pink. Eye-popping, speech-stopping, chair-dropping pink.

Frogger let the kitchen chair fall from his hands as he reached to take the pager from Cigar. He took a quick glance at it, found the power switch, turned it on and checked the tiny display. No messages. Its red READY light pulsed on and off.

"Thanks. I hear she had trouble finding another color."

He started to slip it into his pocket, but Cigar stopped him.

"No, siree. Dolly sez ta wear it on yer belt. Doesn't want it turned off by accident."

Snapping it onto his belt over his right hip, Frogger looked at it forlornly, sorry that he had agreed to be on call 24 hours a day. Sensing his embarrassment, the twins stopped their task of emptying a linen drawer in their search for a tablecloth.

"Frogger's got a pink thing. Frogger's got a pink thing . . . just like a GIRL."

Frogger glared at the twins, but Cigar took control.

"You cheeky little monkeys, hush up. Jes' settle yerselves down, or someone's gonna get their britches burned. Yer supposed ta be gettin' me a cloth for a haircut. If that little pink buzzer starts ta beep, Frogger here is gonna charge off ta save someone's life or somethin'. Then I'll be in charge of you rascals."

Having dumped the contents of two drawers onto the floor, Kenny came up with a large white Irish linen tablecloth and triumphantly waved it around, seemingly oblivious to Cigar's stern lecture. Kerry, on the other hand, eyed Cigar warily, glancing over at the ominous blinking light on Frogger's unmistakably pink pager.

Clippers in one hand and coffee cup in the other, Cigar pushed his way through the back screen door, motioning the boys to drag the huge tablecloth out onto the porch. Frogger followed with the kitchen chair, glancing at the clock above the fireplace. It was almost 10 o'clock. Breakfast was over, and the kitchen was every bit as disastrous-looking as the upstairs bathroom. The morning's phonics and reading lesson was long lost, and it was supposed to be playtime from 10:00 to 11:00, followed by quiet time.

Somehow, the morning schedule had fallen into disarray before it had even got started, and he was at least a haircut away from any chance of getting the day back on track.

31

Just a Trim

"Ahhh, I remember this view," roared Cigar to Kenny, pointing toward the river. "Why, when I wuz yer age, my sister Doris 'n me'd watch the river men float logs downriver to the mills every spring."

He indicated a stretch of rapids that were more rocks than water during the dry summer season and explained to the twins that "come spring, the water jes' boils 'n churns through there. No man or child could survive the poundin' a body'd take gettin' swept over those rocks. That's why folks around these parts called it Widowmaker Falls.

"Mind ya, nothing scared those river rats. Ev'ry spring, this river wuz filled with logs. Men carried long pike poles 'n jumped from log ta log. Rock ta rock. Soaked all the time. Pryin' logs that had got stuck ta break up the jams. My sister 'n me would stand right here watchin'.

"This time o' year, though, it's shallow 'n slow. I'll take ya down there later. Show ya where we used ta catch great big ol' frogs."

"Can't go down there," sang Kerry.

"Mom says we might get drownded," echoed Kenny.

"Ahhh, that's what my mama used ta say," laughed Cigar. "But if ya pay attention 'n know how ta swim, there's no problem."

"We can't swim," the twins confessed.

"Well, yer of an age ta learn," observed Cigar. "First lesson's today. After lunch."

"Let's eat now," shrieked Kenny.

"We can use this as a towel," suggested Kerry, holding up a corner of the tablecloth.

"We'll see about that when it's time. But first, I need a haircut, then I've gotta find me some breakfast."

He shooed the boys over to several small wooden toy chests in one corner of the porch. Each was filled with blocks or trucks or books or puzzles. One had a series of plastic containers, each holding the parts from one of several educational kits. There were bits of a plastic human skeleton, a cross section of a passenger jet and a microscope with dozens of slides. Another contained action figures that transformed into an assortment of trucks, planes and jet boats. Within a minute, they were all empty, the contents spilled halfway across the porch as Kenny got down to the serious business of playing.

Kerry ran to Frogger, who was wrapping one end of the huge tablecloth around Cigar's sunburned neck, using a clothespin to hold it in place.

"Frogger, he dumped out all the toys."

"That's okay. He'll put them back when he's done."

"But we can only use one box of toys at a time. He shouldn't mix them up."

What a dumb rule, thought Frogger, not using blocks and trucks and action characters together. Surely that was why a kid needed lots of toys.

"Don't worry about it, Kerry," he soothed, finally feeling confident that he was able to tell the twins apart. Kenny was the mischievous one, and Kerry was the tattletale. "We'll pick them all up before your parents come home."

Cigar contentedly stared out over the low river falls, oblivious to the twins, while Frogger found an electrical outlet and clipped on a trim guard which would leave the standard half-inch of hair that his father preferred. Cigar's unruly white hair was quite long in places, but Frogger didn't expect any trouble. The twins were busy, and Cigar sat almost motionless. Hesitantly, Frogger eased the buzzing clippers through a thicket of white hair just behind Cigar's right ear. With complete confidence in his young barber, the old man tilted his head forward and to the left, allowing Frogger easier access to the right side of his head. Frogger proceeded without further hesitation, anxious to complete Cigar's trim so that he could get back to the twins' normal routine.

A calm seemed to have settled over the house for the first time since the boys had woken up.

* * *

The peace lasted only about five minutes.

Frogger buzzed the hair off Cigar's head, taking long, straight runs from his neck to his forehead. The hair was toppling gently off Cigar's head, down the tablecloth draped over

34

his shoulders and onto the porch floor. A soft breeze pushed some clumps toward the twins who, unnoticed, were using it as snow around their wooden-block construction project. Cigar's right ear and half of his forehead had just emerged naked to the light of day and Frogger was getting ready to start work on the other side of the old man's head when the little pink beeper attached to his belt began to chirp loudly.

The unexpected sound startled Frogger, who reacted by steering the clippers off course, mowing a path toward Cigar's left ear. Cigar noticed the deviation immediately and broke out of his old-time reverie just as Frogger snapped off the clippers.

The beeper chirped again.

"Sure don't sound pink," observed Cigar. "Could be any color with a twitter like that. Whatcha supposed ta do now?"

Unsure, Frogger pulled the pager off his belt and studied it carefully. He pushed a button, and Mrs. Gilmore's voice came over the tiny speaker loud and clear.

"Frogger, if you can hear me, I need you here as soon as possible. There's a problem at the fire hall, and I've got to get down there. Over and out."

Glancing at the half-trimmed head of Cigar Davis, Frogger hesitated, looking over at the boys, who were staring back from their corner of the porch.

"Sounds like ya'd better hightail it over there," urged Cigar. "Dolly's not one ta be kept waitin'. Ya can finish me up when ya get back." Then, noticing Frogger's glance at the twins, he added, "Don't worry 'bout these little lads. I'll care fer 'em as if they wuz my own."

His half-shorn head gave Cigar Davis the look of a lop-sided sheepdog and did not inspire a great deal of confidence in terms of childcare. But there was an emergency down at the fire hall, and Frogger's help was needed.

Brushing the hair off his T-shirt and jeans, Frogger told the boys to behave for Cigar, then he dashed through the house wondering what trouble had struck Tichburg.

Mrs. Gilmore

Riverview Road was deserted as it always was during the day. There were only six houses along its short length — the Troths' was at the end, nestled among some tall white pine trees at the bottom of a short but steep hill. The street descended sharply just before reaching their house, and all the other homes were arranged along the upper portion of the hill. There was a narrow strip of land between the river and the street, and four of the five houses on the hill had been built with their porches pressed up to the edge of the sidewalk, so as to afford a clear, high view of the river just before it plunged over Widowmaker Falls, behind the Troth house.

Anxious to know what was happening at the fire station, Frogger charged up the hill, running in the middle of the empty roadway, happy to reach its crest, where the sidewalk started in front of Ms. Zariski's place. He jogged more easily as the ground leveled off, careful to jump clear of the bulging parts of the sidewalk where tree roots had spread underneath and forced the concrete into an uneven series of rolling waves and treacherous cracks.

Tearing past the McAvoys' house, he waved quickly at Barney, their barking beagle, who had taken on the responsibility of announcing the passing of each car and pedestrian on Riverview. The McAvoys blocked off both ends of their front porch to keep Barney at home while they were at work, but Barney stayed on the porch only when the mood struck him. The rest of the time, he managed to clamber over the railing and down the stairs, free to wander Tichburg at will, nosing his way through the village until midafternoon, when he instinctively returned to his porch lookout — long before the McAvoys returned from work.

Next came Frogger's own little white house, its clapboard siding peeling as it had been for the 10 years that they had owned it. His parents had bought the house cheaply when they moved into Tichburg and had been renovating it as time and money allowed, but their progress was slow, and consequently, the exterior of the house showed little improvement.

On the far side of his own house, a high, thick wall of cedar hedge shielded the Knowltons' house from view until he was almost at the mouth of his own driveway. Skidding on the gravel that spilled onto the concrete sidewalk from the Archibalds' unpaved driveway, he glanced to the right and breathed a sigh of relief. Nicky Knowlton's car was not at home.

The Knowltons, a nice couple nearing retirement age, had had their son Nicky late in life and had proceeded to spoil him shamelessly. Predictably, their beloved Nicky had not responded well to the extra attention. For all his 18 years, he had been given everything he demanded, a fact that had done little to improve his Neanderthal charms. A loud junk-food-driven chubster with pimply skin, long, greasy hair and a black Camaro, Nicky liked to make life miserable for everyone around him. Frogger had spent most of his life trying to escape Nicky's notice and had largely succeeded. For his part, Nicky seemed to assume that their next-door-neighbor status required some restraint and gave Frogger only passing attention.

Frogger was used to Nicky's taunting "Yoo, Froggee. Rivet-rivet-rivet" whenever they passed on Tichburg's streets, but he had never suffered the harassment common to the less fortunate Tichburgers whose existence had caught Nicky's attention. Aside from an occasional dead robin in their yard, courtesy of Nicky's unerring aim with an air gun, and the inevitable anonymous barrage of rotten fruit at Hallowe'en, living beside the Knowltons had, so far, been pretty bearable through Nicky's juvenile-delinquent stage.

At last, he reached the near corner of Dolly Gilmore's yard. Hopping over the low stone wall that marked the limits of her neat lawn, he raced toward the steps that led up to her porch and its side kitchen door. Mrs. Gilmore was standing at the kitchen door watching his progress, a stopwatch in hand.

"Four minutes, thirty-seven seconds," she announced as he reached the screen door. "Not bad for the first time out. If you had your bicycle, you'd probably cut that time in half. I figure with your bike, you'll never be more than five or six minutes away no matter where you are in the village."

Gulping air, Frogger nodded wordlessly, allowing Mrs. Gilmore to continue.

"There's really no emergency, but I could use your help for about 15 minutes. I have to run down to the fire hall because the number-two tanker has been leaking water the past couple of days and making a mess all over the floor. The truck depot is sending someone over from Wamble to take a look at it. I have to run down, empty the tanks before he comes and then hang around until he's through looking or fixing or whatever he's going to do."

Mrs. Gilmore was quite a talker and liked to give exact details about everything, so Frogger stood listening, catching his breath and wondering where he fit into the plan. If she was going to be at the fire station, she didn't need him to monitor her phone up here because the phone rang in both places.

"Well, I promised Birdie Pickett I was going to enter some pies in the Harvest Fair bake contest tomorrow, and I was a bit late getting them into the oven this morning because that old Cigar Davis showed up just as I was getting ready to roll out my crusts. He was looking for breakfast and a haircut, if you can imagine. At 7:30! I was still wearing my housecoat when he just walked into my kitchen."

As she spoke, Mrs. Gilmore laid down her stopwatch and was working away to loosen the knot on her apron as she wandered deeper into the kitchen. When it was almost free, she continued.

"I decided to send him down to see you, just to get him out of my hair. I was going to phone over to the Troths to warn you he was coming, but I still don't have their number. It's

40

unlisted, if you can believe that. So I tried the pager but guessed that you didn't have it turned on. I finally just told the old fool to go ahead and to try not to scare you but to introduce himself at the door and tell you to call me if you weren't sure who he was.

"When you didn't phone, I figured you hadn't been paying attention to the strangers-at-the-door part of the babysitting course or else he just walked in unannounced."

Frogger affirmed her latter suspicion with a sheepish grin.

"Well, no harm done, but that man does have a way of just wandering into people's daily lives. Haven't seen him in 15 years, since he announced that he was retiring in Florida, right after his wife Hazel died. Most of us figured we'd seen the last of him, then in he walks to my kitchen, as if he had never left Riverview Road. It was like seeing a ghost — a loud, hungry ghost at that."

"He's a pretty friendly guy but messy," said Frogger.

"Oh, my, he's not messing up that lovely house down there, is he? Well, of course he is, if he is the same Cigar Davis that drove poor Hazel crazy for all those years. That man should be living in a barn the way he behaves."

Frogger was about to suggest that he return to the Troths' immediately, but Mrs. Gilmore cut him off.

"I have four pies in the oven right now that won't be done for another 15 minutes. I need you here to pull them out to cool on the counter. They're lemon pies, and the meringue will burn if you leave them in one minute too long. So keep an eye on them and pull them out the minute they turn the teeniest bit brown. You know how a lemon pie is supposed to look.

"Then, when they are done, I suggest you race right back to the bottom of the street and send Cigar over to the fire station where we can find something for him to do to keep the peace. I would have asked him to tend these pies except he probably would have eaten one. Plus I think he's overdue for a bath."

A Barrow of Trouble

Frogger followed Mrs. Gilmore to the kitchen door, taking her apron as she handed it to him.

"Be sure to use oven mitts, and don't forget to turn the oven off when you're done," she instructed as she walked out the door and across the porch. "Wouldn't do for the fire chief to have her house burned down — especially by her assistant."

She paused on the bottom step and turned. "Thanks a lot for your help, Frogger. I'll try to get a different color of pager for you next month when the ElectroMart gets in its next shipment. And bring those little Troth terrors down to the fire hall later if you want. We'll let them climb on the engines and have some real fun."

Frogger started to tell her that the twins were not allowed to climb but thought better of it, knowing Mrs. Gilmore's opinion of Mr. and Mrs. Troth. Her old cat Turnip had disappeared the week the Troths moved in, and she was convinced that in addition to their sins of being rich, standoffish and city-bred, they were also cat killers who drove their big, red truck too fast and too recklessly. Although Frogger rightly assumed that no one had ever asked the Troths whether they had run over old Turnip, the regulars down at Birdie Pickett's Lucky Dollar store had convicted the Troths of the crime on the flimsiest of circumstantial evidence: (1) Turnip had been a constant presence along Riverview Road for 14 years, and (2) her disappearance was too close to the arrival of the Troths to be a coincidence.

Frogger watched Mrs. Gilmore's short, round shape hustle down the sidewalk to the corner, where she turned left onto Main Street and headed across the bridge into the village center. When she was in a hurry, she moved quickly, with an uneven running-walk that consisted of several short jogging steps followed by a slightly slower walk, which lasted for about another half-dozen steps, before she started her jog again. She leaned forward with her shoulders and pumped her arms like a speed walker but set her feet down gingerly, as if she were walking on hot coals. Although there was no doubt that she had sore feet, she was very fast for a 70-year-old.

Frogger had been accompanying Mrs. Gilmore around Tichburg since he had been old enough to walk, first as a preschooler, when she had been his daytime babysitter, and later as a friend. But he found it hard to walk with her when she was in a hurry — not because she was too fast for him but because she was constantly changing her pace. It seemed that he was always a step or two out of sync — speeding up as she slowed down and slowing down just as she broke into her jog.

These days, he tended to jump on his bicycle and simply ride ahead to meet her wherever they were headed.

He wandered out onto the swinging love seat that graced the far corner of the front portion of the porch. Nearly all the old houses in Tichburg had originally had front porches when they were built in the 19th century, but many were now tumbledown or had been demolished because they were too expensive to repair. Only a few dozen old porches remained on the houses of Tichburg, and several of them had been closed in with doors and large windows to give their owners protection from the wind and snow of winter. And while every house on Riverview Road still boasted a porch, Mrs. Gilmore's was the most impressive one. In fact, with its fine wooden posts, carved rails and fancy trim, it was easily the nicest one in Tichburg.

Mrs. Gilmore's house had been built in the 1860s by her great-grandfather, a wealthy man who had owned one of Tichburg's three mills. He had set his beautiful brick house slightly back from Main Street so that all passersby entering the village could look across its rolling lawn and call out a respectful greeting without feeling obliged to enter into a long conversation. This had been important to the old man because many of those people driving their buggies down Main Street were his employees, and in those days, mill owners were not expected to socialize with common workers.

Riverview Road had been extended over the years, and five other houses had been built along it, each overlooking the river, but only the Davis house, now owned by the Troths, had been as large as the Gilmore house. The Davises had been much more reclusive and had chosen not to flaunt their wealth to casual passersby, preferring peace and quiet at the end of a secluded street to a daily parade of admirers who wanted to call out their hellos.

The porch upon which Frogger sat lounging on the swing wrapped around three sides of the house. There was the Main Street viewing area to the east, where he was now; the Riverview greeting area to the north, which also afforded a good look at the original limestone Gilmore Woolen Mill across the river; and a more private side-porch area to the west, which was shaded from view of Nicky Knowlton's house by a wall of thick vines called Dutchman's-pipe.

It seemed to Frogger that he had practically grown up on this veranda (the word that Mrs. Gilmore preferred to use when she referred to her porch). From the time he was 2 years old, when his mother had started her hospital job and began leaving him with Mrs. Gilmore each workday, Frogger had been observing the traffic as it eased by along Main Street, waving to pedestrians and drivers alike and watching school buses bring older kids into school each morning until he himself was old enough to attend Tichburg Public School.

It was on this porch that Mrs. Gilmore had helped him conquer his fear of thunderstorms almost eight years ago. The first time she heard him begin to whimper at the sound of thunder, Mrs. Gilmore had bundled him up on the porch swing and taught him how to watch the sky for the flash of lightning that always preceded the next crash of thunder and count the seconds between lightning and noise to judge the storm's approach. It was a wonderful porch that allowed its

46

occupants a ringside seat on village life in all kinds of weather, and Frogger loved it.

Checking his watch, he judged that he had another seven minutes before he had to pull the pies out of the oven. He was about to pick up a nearby copy of *Fire Safety* magazine when he heard the high-pitched laughter of Kenny and Kerry. He jumped to his feet, ran to the west side of the porch and peered down the street. Sure enough, he saw Cigar Davis pushing the twins down the middle of Riverview Road in a rickety old wheelbarrow. The wheel was loose on its axle and occasionally wobbled crazily to one side or the other, forcing the wheelbarrow to veer off unexpectedly. Whenever this happened, the Troth twins squealed with delight while Cigar warned them to settle down.

"You pups are gonna tip this ol' bucket down-side-up if ya aren't careful. Now set still 'n enjoy the scenery."

But being reprimanded by an old man with half a haircut and a long, bushy beard just sent them into greater hysterics. They were having a wonderful time. Cigar was making slow but steady progress with his squirming load, but without the aid of his cane, his own unsteady gait added an extra bounce to each forward step that seemed to be a more serious threat to stability than the fidgeting of the twins. As they pulled closer to Mrs. Gilmore's house, the pair waved wildly at Frogger, anxious for him to see their approach.

"I needed ta come up 'n get some o' Dolly's tools, 'n these young 'uns couldn't keep pace with me," called Cigar. "So I borrowed this ol' barrow from up against yer neighbor's house. With this blessed wobblin' wheel, it sure ain't worth stealin'."

47

Frogger didn't know what to say and merely waved, which in turn inspired Kenny to clamber over Kerry to get to the prime waving position. The maneuver was unwise, and although Cigar fought valiantly to keep the wheelbarrow upright, the old wheel collapsed onto its side — sending the twins flying. Kerry landed on top of Kenny, driving his knees into his brother's back before rolling gently off onto the grass that grew beside the roadway. Kenny was not so lucky. His knees and hands hit the gravel shoulder, and the added weight of Kerry landing on him drove his bare skin hard against the small stones.

Kenny started to cry immediately, and Kerry, sensing that he had been responsible for his brother's pain, joined in.

Frogger leaped off the porch and ran the short distance to the scene of the accident. By the time he arrived, Cigar had retrieved his cane from underneath the wheelbarrow, rolled Kenny onto his back and tucked him under one arm. Frogger scooped up Kerry and followed Cigar to the porch steps, where they both sat down to survey the damage. Kerry was still howling full blast, while Kenny had toned down his ruckus to steady sobs. Cigar was carefully plucking bits of gravel and dirt from Kenny's palms, gently praising the boy for being so brave.

"S'not too bad, little fella. She'll burn 'n sting fer a spell, but it'll soon ease up. Frogger, trot on in 'n get a clean wet rag so's we can tidy this boy up 'n get a better look."

Still holding Kerry, Frogger jumped up, raced into the house and rummaged around the kitchen until he found a washcloth. He quickly ran it under hot water and hurried back outside. Kerry had spotted a plate of peanut-butter cookies on their way past the counter and had grabbed one before Frogger could stop him. He quickly quit crying, deciding to munch sadly instead, so Frogger went back and got one for Kenny.

Within a few minutes, Cigar and Frogger had cleaned up Kenny's scrapes and stopped the trickles of blood that had marked the worst-damaged areas. He had wriggled off the top step and was tentatively exploring the porch, limping carefully with each step while slowly munching his cookie. Kerry had already disappeared around the corner to check out the view of Main Street.

"Oh, we had some fine times on this here porch," breathed Cigar as he climbed the steps to follow Kenny's progress. "Dolly's grandpa lived here when I wuz jes' a bit older than you, Frogger — Dolly wuz just a bitty baby then — 'n he knew how to lay on a party. Christmas. Easter. Just about any ol' time. He 'n his father both liked ta entertain folks, least-ways the folks they thought wuz important. 'N while all the fine grown-up guests were inside visitin', we'd be out here courtin' 'n havin' our own brand o' fun. The young 'uns, like yer twins there, would be scurryin' in 'n out 'n all about."

By this time, Kenny had found Kerry on the porch swing, and although it was wide enough to seat quadruplets, he was in the midst of forcing his brother off the seat when Frogger's pink pager beeped into action.

"Frogger, I just thought I had better remind you to watch those pies. Don't want them to burn. Over and out."

Stuck

Leaving the Troth twins with Cigar, Frogger raced into the kitchen to the unmistakable smell of scorched meringue. He slipped on the oven mitts, whipped open the oven door and was relieved that no flames or charred remains awaited him. But it was clear that these four pies would not be winning any blue ribbons at the Harvest Fair's Kitchen 'N Craft Shed.

Each one that he hauled out and placed atop the stove was just a little darker than the previous one, and not even the first pie to be rescued was worthy of an honorable mention. While they should have boasted a wavy topping of white meringue with lightly tanned peaks, this quartet of pies was distinctly crispy brown in color with blackened wave tips. Even the crusts were slightly burnt.

Frogger dejectedly reached across the pies to turn off the

oven and stood for a moment staring at them. Mrs. Gilmore made the best pies in Tichburg, and he had just become responsible for the ruination of her next entry in the meringue category. He pulled off the oven mitts, picked up a butter knife and tried to scrape the scorched film of brown and black off the least burnt pie but succeeded only in ripping a large crater in the coating. It was like trying to shape a burnt marshmallow; the meringue was still hot and very sticky, and it clung stubbornly to the blade. A hole the size of a quarter quickly grew many times larger as Frogger struggled to spread the meringue back in place. A bright yellow patch of lemon filling clearly indicated the attempted repair, and Frogger gave up, knowing that he was just making matters worse.

Unsure of how he was going to break the bad news to Mrs. Gilmore, Frogger slowly returned to the porch. That's when he decided that he would take the boys down to the fire station and explain about the pies in person. After that, he would get back to Cigar's haircut. By then, it would be noon and time for lunch, followed by the twins' rest time, during which he could tidy up the kitchen. And the bathroom. And the back porch. Babysitting was a lot more work than he had ever imagined.

Rounding the corner, he was surprised to see Cigar down on his hands and knees, hovering over top of Kerry as Kenny sat giggling on the porch swing. At first, Frogger assumed that they were wrestling, although there was no laughter coming from either of the combatants, and as he drew closer, he realized that not all of Kerry's body was visible. Beyond the shoulders, his body just seemed to end.

51

Cigar heard his footsteps and chuckled sheepishly. "This little fella's got more speed than brains," he said. "One minute, he's listenin' to a tale 'bout the night I fell over backwards off this very porch tryin' to impress Mabel Chalmers, 'n the next thing I know, the poor gaffer's got his head jammed in betwixt the rails here."

"I wampf ooot," came Kerry's muffled voice.

"He wants out," translated Kenny, slipping off the swing.

"Back up there, ya young imp," commanded Cigar in a stern voice. Looking up at Frogger, he explained, "This 'un keeps nippin' over fer a wee game of footsie with his brother's hind end, so I sat him down there."

Remembering the long list of emergency phone numbers that the Troths had left him, Frogger opted for the more typical Tichburg response — he would call Mrs. Gilmore at the fire station. But before departing for the phone, he squeezed down beside Kerry, easing gently past Cigar, so as to assess the situation. He knew that Mrs. Gilmore would have questions for him, and he wanted to make sure he had all the answers.

Recalling the standard emergency steps, he swung into action, patting Kerry's shoulder.

"I wampf ooot," repeated Kerry.

"I know you do," Frogger replied. "Help is going to be here any minute. I just have to make sure you are all right."

"I amfnot all ripe. My head is stufpt."

He was having trouble speaking clearly, because his face was down tight against the bottom piece of the railing.

Frogger offered him reassurance.

"You'll be out of there in a few minutes. Just don't talk. Can you breathe all right?"

No answer.

"I said, 'Can you breathe?' "

No answer.

Panicking a bit, Frogger shook Kerry's shoulder gently. "Are you all right? Speak to me."

"You toll me nof to talk," Kerry replied.

"Oh, right. Good boy. You just keep still, and we'll get you out in a minute."

Frogger knew that injured children should not be moved in emergency situations — and there was certainly no threat of that in this case. He also knew that the victim was to be made as comfortable as possible, which also seemed impossible. He decided to check Kerry from the other side of the rail and hoisted his leg over the top rail of the porch.

His babysitter guide warned about putting yourself at risk while attempting a rescue, but the porch was only three feet off the ground, and there were lots of bushes and flowers below to break his fall. Besides, the greatest danger to his health right now was going to be Mrs. Troth — unless Mrs. Gilmore got really angry over the burnt pies.

To get a closer look, Frogger lowered himself down until he was level with Kerry's small head. The youngster had got his head halfway through the bars but had become stuck as he had tried to squeeze his ears through. Frogger's fingers gently massaged the crown of Kerry's head, then gave him a little pat. He looked up at Cigar, who, worried, was running his fingers through the long half of his own hair.

"You go in and call Mrs. Gilmore down at the fire station," said Frogger. "Tell her that Kerry is conscious and his pulse is good and strong. And that he seems to be able to breathe. But he is really stuck tight, so she had better bring the rescue truck."

When Cigar had disappeared into the house, Frogger climbed back across the railing and sat down next to Kerry, patting his back and reassuring him that everything would soon be all right. And then, turning to Kenny, he started talking to him, knowing how important it was to keep both of the twins calm.

"We're going to have some visitors in a fire truck any minute now, guys," he explained. "And they'll have equipment to help us out. Firefighters are prepared for any kind of emergency."

"Any kind?" asked Kenny.

"Sure."

"That's good, because I think Kerry might have to go to the bathroom."

Rescue

The Tichburg Emergency Rescue Van lumbered into the drive-way within a few minutes of Cigar's call to the fire station. Mrs. Gilmore was at the wheel with Randy Timmerman beside her in the passenger seat, and she honked the horn and waved to Frogger as the truck rolled to a stop. Randy hopped out first, ran to open the double back doors and clambered in to get some equipment. Mrs. Gilmore climbed out and hustled up the porch steps to examine the situation.

"How's this little pumpkin head doing?" she asked, squat-ting down beside Kerry. "Don't you worry, dear, we're going to get you out of there in two shakes of a lamb's tail."

"I wampf ooot," came the boy's reply.

"He wants out," explained Kenny from the swing, anxious to take part in the unfolding drama. "He's been there for a long time."

"I'm sure he does," agreed Mrs. Gilmore. "And he will be

55

out very soon." Turning to Frogger, she ordered, "Run into the kitchen and get the bottle of vegetable oil I keep on the counter near the stove."

"Okay. I'm really sorry about this. I didn't . . . ," he started to explain, but she cut him off.

"Don't you worry, either. Everything is going to work out just fine. These things happen — especially when Cigar Davis is around."

Frogger tore into the kitchen and almost knocked over Cigar, who was easing past the doorway. He had been watching the rescue on the porch from a front window and was in full retreat.

"That woman'll blame anythin' 'n everythin' on me, given the chance, but I had nuthin' — not a thing — ta do with this. So I'm just gonna borrow those tools I came fer 'n head out 'fore she decides ta blame me fer Noah's flood too.

"I've a little job ta do, 'n when I'm done 'n you boys're back home, we'll finish my haircut. I've gotta start lookin' fer a place ta stay. 'N a job. Nobody'll take me on when I look like some half-shaved ape-man."

And with that, he disappeared from sight down the hallway that led to the garage attached to the back of the house.

By the time Frogger rushed back to the railing with the bottle of vegetable oil in hand, Randy Timmerman was standing there in his big, floppy boots and firefighter's helmet. He had unloaded a huge assortment of tools, including a chain saw that was balanced on top of a plastic tub filled with crowbars, bolt cutters and a small hydraulic jack.

"Now, Dolly, if you just slip on back, I can nip the top off that rail, and the little guy'll be out of there in no time."

"With what?" challenged Mrs. Gilmore. "That chain saw? Even if you didn't accidentally cut off anything else, the poor little tyke would be traumatized for the rest of his life. There is no need to be quite so dramatic."

Turning back to Kerry, she patted his back and told him not to worry.

"Is he going to cut off Kerry's head with that?" asked Kenny, pointing to the large chain saw now in Randy's hands. "I don't like that man."

Frogger handed the bottle of vegetable oil to the fire chief and slipped over to the porch swing to sit with Kenny, who, for a change, seemed genuinely concerned about his brother's fate.

For his part, Kerry had started to howl. Mrs. Gilmore gave Randy a withering glare and removed the cap from the bottle, talking softly to the trapped boy.

"Don't you mind anybody but me, Kerry Troth," she soothed, as she poured oil into the palms of her hands and reached through the rails to rub it onto his head. Tipping the bottle carefully, she drizzled some more oil down the insides of the rails and over Kerry's ears and neck. Listening to her reminded Frogger of the countless times she had gently tended his cuts and bruises when he was small. But, he thought, he had never been stupid enough to stick his head through any railings.

"Now, we are just going to slip that head of yours back my way and then get you a cookie."

"I likth cookeeth," Kerry managed to say.

"He likes cookies," explained Kenny. "And so do I."

Mrs. Gilmore reached through the railing and gave the top

of Kerry's head a gentle push, but nothing happened. She pushed again, a bit harder this time, but still there was no movement. She poured some more oil out of the bottle, and carefully tried to move his head up and down to work the lubricant between his ears and the railings. But his head didn't budge.

"Randy, you go down into the flowerbed so that you can give him a little push straight on. And get those tools out of our way. Frogger, you come closer, in case I need you to pull."

Watching Randy wade clumsily through the flowerbed in his oversized boots, she cautioned him to be a bit more careful. "You don't have to kill all my pansies on your way through there, you know. It wouldn't hurt to leave half of them standing."

Then, with Randy pushing the top of Kerry's head with one hand and Mrs. Gilmore pulling on his small shoulders, they tried again — unsuccessfully. Kerry began to whimper and kick his legs. As he squirmed, his head moved — but the wrong way — and his skull advanced even farther into the pinch of the rails.

"Well, either we'll have to just give him a good yank and push," offered Randy, "or I can get him out with this." And having said that, he lifted the massive chain saw from the bushes behind him and fired it up full throttle.

The saw's noisy engine kicked into life and wailed dangerously. Horrified, Kenny fell off the porch swing and landed against Frogger, who lost his balance and crashed into Mrs. Gilmore, who was struggling to jump up for a clearer view of Randy. As the three of them fell into a jumble around Kerry, the startled boy desperately wrenched his head from the rails.

He was free — and terrified.

"Make him go away," he sobbed, pointing at Randy, who was setting the chain saw down on the edge of the lawn after turning off its engine. Then, rubbing his oil-slicked head and his red ears, Kerry added, "My brain hurts."

Mrs. Gilmore was furious. She untangled herself from the knot of twins and Frogger, picked up Kerry and turned to the sheepish-looking firefighter below her.

"Randy Timmerman, you load those tools into that truck right now and head on back to the fire hall. I'll deal with you later. You should be ashamed of yourself, frightening this youngster clear out of his mind. Now get!"

Frogger had never seen her so angry before, and evidently, neither had Randy, for the young firefighter picked up the tub of tools and forlornly headed for the safety of the van. Halfway there, he stopped and started to explain his actions.

"I just thought a little scare would work, and it did . . . ," he stammered, but Mrs. Gilmore was having none of it.

"I said, 'Get,' " she ordered, then turned her attention back to the twins and Frogger. "I swear, a bag of hammers has more sense than that man. Now, let's get you cleaned up and find some cookies."

While the others went inside, Frogger paused to watch Randy throw the tools into the back of the van and slink around to the cab. It was true that Randy Timmerman lacked a certain amount of common sense, but everyone in Tichburg liked him, most of all the kids. In fact, Randy was about the biggest kid in Tichburg. He was easygoing and seemed to have devoted his life to becoming the village's unofficial clown. Twenty-five years old and unmarried, he had worked for Rollie Estabrook's construction company since he graduated from high school, and there wasn't a tool or piece of equipment that he could not operate. He still lived with his parents but spent all his time working — and entertaining everyone around him. When he had time off, he could be found at the fire station, washing and polishing the trucks and tending to the equipment.

The reason every kid in Tichburg liked Randy was because he drove the school bus mornings and afternoons each school day, slipping away from his regular job for an hour at a time so as to shuttle the area's kids back and forth to school. The atmosphere on board his bus was riotous — pure pandemonium — and while no one was ever allowed out of his or her seat while the bus was moving, each trip was spectacular fun. Randy had never been able to sit still or keep quiet himself, so whenever the kids were too quiet, he would burst into song or call out good-natured insults to whomever he could spot in his big overhead mirror until he had restored the hullabaloo to full volume. The teachers claimed that they could hear his bus approaching the school from two blocks away. But they never complained, because Randy's young passengers had usually burned up their daily dose of silliness by the time they got to the classroom.

Yet as Frogger watched Randy climb into the cab of the emergency van, there was no sense of fun in him at all. He backed down the driveway carefully and headed slowly off to the fire station.

Kitchen Confessions

Frogger did not stay long in Mrs. Gilmore's kitchen. The fire chief had been in a spitting mood because of the chain saw, and he doubted whether she was going to be any happier when she found her scorched pies. Besides, it was almost 11:30, and the twins were supposed to be on a strict schedule. So far, he had missed nearly every part of their routine; lunch was less than 40 minutes away, and Cigar would be waiting for him to finish the haircut.

He declined her offer of a cookie and a glass of milk and took up a position near the stove, where the pies sat.

"I had some trouble with those pies," he explained. "I forgot about them when I saw Cigar Davis pushing the twins up the road in a wheelbarrow."

"Him again," Mrs. Gilmore harrumphed.

"It wasn't really his fault. He was playing with the kids, and the wheelbarrow's wheel was really wobbly, and they fell out and . . . ," he was interrupted again.

"Someone is always getting hurt when Cigar Davis is around. That man is a walking disaster zone."

"Well, anyway, after we got the twins calmed down, I noticed the pies were starting to burn. Then I tried to fix one of them but just made a big hole in it and . . . ." He was talking faster now, worried that if he slowed down, he would start crying or something before he could finish his story. But Mrs. Gilmore waved for him to be silent.

"There's no serious harm done. I shouldn't have asked you to mind the pies anyway. You had an important job to do, and I took you away from it. You're only supposed to be on call for official fire-department business, and I had you baking pies for the fair. Why, having someone else tending my competition pies was practically cheating anyway. I don't know what I was thinking. It's selfishness, that's what it is. Selfishness, plain and simple." She paused to catch her breath and looked at Frogger kindly.

"In a way, everything that has happened has been my own fault. I never should have sent Cigar to the Troths' house in the first place. I might as well have sent the devil himself down there."

The twins sat quietly at the table, solemnly listening to every word. Kerry, his dark hair and forehead slick with vegetable oil, gingerly touched one red ear and piped up: "I'm sorry I stuck my head between the railings. That was dumb."

"And I'm sorry I kicked him when he was stuck," added Kenny. "Twice."

He glared at Kerry, warning him not to try to outconfess him.

62

"Well, everyone has survived the ordeal," concluded Mrs. Gilmore. She rose from the table, gave Frogger a grandmotherly hug and looked down at her four ruined pies.

"I'll tend to those later. I had better get back to the fire hall to see how that repair is coming along and have a serious talk with Randy Timmerman — explain a few facts about small boys and chain saws."

And with that, Frogger ushered the twins out of the house and down the street. Past the collapsed wheelbarrow, abandoned in front of the Knowltons' house. Past the McAvoys' barking dog, who left his porch to get a good sniff of Kerry's head. And down the steep hill to the house in which Cigar Davis had grown up.

Bubbles and Banging

There was no immediate sign of Cigar when Frogger and the twins entered the house, so they checked the kitchen and the back porch in search of him. Certainly, there was clear evidence that he had been here earlier. Coffee still dripped across the kitchen counter, and drawers had been pulled out and emptied onto the floor. Wisps of white hair floated across the porch, gently wafting from the pile that surrounded Mrs. Troth's good linen tablecloth. Some of it had settled into the flowerbeds at the base of the porch, adding a feathery whiteness to a bed of purple periwinkle. There were also clear signs that the boys had engaged in a toy-tossing match during Frogger's absence, for a variety of action heroes peered out from the foliage below.

Frogger sighed and grabbed the twins before they could

return to the massive pile of toys spread across the porch.

"Kerry, I've got to clean you up before lunch. Once we get that oil slick off your head, we can eat."

Reasoning that dish detergent was supposed to be good at washing grease away, he steered Kerry toward the kitchen sink, standing him on a wooden chair so that he could reach the faucet. As warm water gushed from the spout, Frogger checked the temperature twice, then eased the boy's head under the stream. Ignoring the squawks of protest, he lathered Kerry up with the green liquid soap until his head was covered in suds.

"Keep your eyes shut tight," he commanded. "We'll rinse the soap off in a second."

Feeling left out, Kenny pushed a chair up to the counter beside them and used a frying-pan spatula to scoop up a mound of bubbles. Waving it frantically, he succeeded in launching the bubbles across the room.

"Hey, I want to do that too," whined Kerry, his eyes wide open despite the risk of the soap.

"So just shake your head, bubble brain," suggested Kenny.

Kerry decided to ignore the insult and gave his head a terrific shake, spattering soap all over Frogger. Soon, the counter and floor were a soapy mess, and the boys were shrieking gleefully — Frogger included. Turning it into a game, he coaxed Kerry to put his head back under the faucet for a thorough rinse and then obliged Kenny by doing the same to him. By the time they were finished, everyone was soaking wet and soapy puddles dotted the floor, but Kerry's oily head was as clean as a whistle, and the trauma that had taken place on Mrs. Gilmore's porch was forgotten.

* * *

When the soapy free-for-all ended and Frogger had turned off the tap, he started to dry the boys' heads using some dish towels he found in a pile of linens on the floor. It was nearly noon, and it seemed that at least the twins' lunch would be served on time. Things were beginning to look manageable again when a distant *thwack* sounded overhead.

Thwack. Thwack. Thwack. Three muffled thuds that sounded as if . . . as if someone were pounding a wall with a . . . with a sledgehammer! Frogger shushed the twins and stood near the front hallway to listen harder. Two more thuds indicated that whatever it was, it was upstairs. Maybe on the third floor.

Certain that it must be Cigar Davis, Frogger felt no fear about investigating further, although he suddenly had a queasy feeling in the pit of his stomach. If the old man was up to something, it was bound to be more trouble for Frogger. Taking each twin by a hand, he crept up the 20 stairs to the second-floor landing. The interiors of most of the rooms were visible from the top step, and none of them offered a clue as to the source of the racket.

Thwack. Thwack. Thwack. Thwack. Thwack.

The burst of noise seemed to be coming from two directions at once. Above their heads, the ceiling shook, while at the end of the hall, a closed door rattled on its hinges. Certainly the sound was louder upstairs, and it seemed to be emanating from behind a narrow door located between the Troths' bedroom and the bathroom.

66

"What's in there?" whispered Frogger, pointing to the source of the noise.

"Stairs," answered Kenny.

"We're not allowed to go up them," stated Kerry.

"Where do they go?" asked Frogger.

"The attic," replied Kenny.

"Mommy's attic," added Kerry. "No one is allowed to go up there."

"Is it a ghost?" asked Kenny. "It's probably a ghost — and he's going to get you." He turned to his brother and made a scary face, stretching his mouth wide and bugging out his eyes.

"Nah. I think it's just Mr. Davis," said Frogger bravely. "Let's go on up and see what he's doing."

"I like him," offered Kerry. "He's lots of fun."

Followed by the boys, Frogger walked resolutely to the closed door and gently turned the knob and pulled. It was stuck, so he took a firmer grip and yanked hard. There were two more thuds overhead before the door flew open and a white cloud of dust came floating down on top of them. Frogger got the worst of it and began to cough violently, while the twins squeezed past him and charged up the steps through the haze. Frogger followed blindly, bent over so that he could feel his way up the steep steps. The stairs turned sharply to the right and then straightened out. As Frogger climbed, the cloud diminished, and he could begin to make out what must have been Mrs. Troth's office.

Beams of sunshine from two skylights illuminated the room, capturing the floating motes of dust in long, high columns, while the rest of the room was lost in shadow.

Peering hard, Frogger made out the shape of Cigar Davis, flanked by two smaller figures. Everything was covered in a fine white powder, including the twins, whose damp hair and skin were caked with it. As he approached the trio, Frogger spotted a large crowbar and a sledgehammer next to a gaping hole in Mrs. Troth's clean white plaster wall.

"Boys, I found what I wuz lookin' fer," Cigar rejoiced. He was in high spirits, oblivious to the destruction around him. The twins huddled closer. "When I wuz young — 'bout Frogger's age there — I had a secret hidin' place up here. My folks stored things in the narrow crawl spaces behind them walls, 'n I'd crawl in there with a flashlight 'n hide when I wanted ta be by m'self — which was fairly often. I always seemed ta be in some kinda trouble."

The twins nodded understandingly. Certainly Frogger had no difficulty believing that the old man had upset his parents on a regular basis. Probably half the village was ready to lynch him at any given time.

"Well, my daddy 'n mama kept boxes 'n trunks full of ol' clothes 'n pictures 'n bits o' furniture up here, so I decided ta hide away a few treasures of my own. I found a loose floorboard in the crawl space, 'n I kept all sorts o' things down there, where nobody'd ever find 'em."

Cigar beamed over at Frogger, assuming that his story was so logical, no one could question the wisdom of bashing a huge hole in a newly renovated room in a house which did not belong to him.

"Yessir, Frogger, when I saw that picture of my Hazel hangin' in the front hall, I got ta thinkin' I'd left a lotta things behind with Doris when I headed South years ago. Sure 'nuff, all those ol' pictures 'n things are gone — heaven knows where, cuz I've just seen the one so far — but I started wonderin' if some of my boyhood treasures weren't still tucked away up here in my secret hidin' place."

At the word treasure, Kenny and Kerry moved in even closer to their newfound hero.

"You found treasure in Mommy's special room?" whispered an awestruck Kerry.

"Is it ours now?" asked Kenny.

"Oh, no, siree," laughed Cigar. "Yer folks may've bought the house 'n all the ol' junk in it, but I still own all the secrets."

Turning to Frogger, he picked up a bright yellow Space Flight Starship with two headlights that he had found in the twins' room and directed its beams into the dark looming hole, big enough for three or four kids to climb through at once.

"Now, if ya'd do me the honor of takin' a peek, Frogger, we'll finish up this treasure hunt so's we can get back ta the barberin' business. My ol' body's just not up ta crawlin' around like it used ta be."

Behind the Wall

While he was quite conscious of the destruction and dust around him, Frogger was quick to accept the Space Flight Starship flashlight. He was certainly interested to see what Cigar had hidden away so many years ago, but he also knew that the sooner he recovered the old man's boyhood treasures, the sooner they could start to clean up the mess. Mrs. Troth was due back in just two hours, and even though he could not patch up this huge hole in her office wall, he could at least have the rest of the house tidied up.

He ducked through the hole in the low wall, stepping gingerly into the inky blackness. The crawl space ran along the length of the east side of the house. Its low ceiling was steeply sloped, following the pitch of the roof, and there was barely room to walk crouched over. An adult would have had to crawl on hands and knees, but Frogger was short for his age and had no trouble as long as he remained bent at the waist and knees.

The space was quite narrow, and Frogger reached out his arms to feel both walls at the same time. It was dusty, and cobwebs hung down from the rafters, giving a creepy feel to the place. He aimed the toy's headlights ahead of him, but he saw nothing. No storage boxes. No pieces of furniture. No treasure chests. No bats. And no monsters.

Turning back toward the hole, he could see that the wall had once had a low door framed into it but that the Troths had removed it and covered the opening with drywall. Light leaked in through two small holes on either side of the opening where Cigar had punched through the wall during his search for the original doorway. Suddenly, Cigar's head and shoulders poked through the old door frame, a twin's head flanking him on each side.

"Great hidin' space, eh?" he cackled. "Don't know why these new folks filled in that doorway. No sense to it. Would've been a great place fer these little gaffers ta play. I imagine they'll have plenty o' reason ta want ta squirrel away from trouble as they get older." He laughed at his joke, and the twins solemnly nodded in agreement.

"So how do I find the hiding space? Is it under this floor?" asked Frogger, aiming the light down toward his feet.

"Yessiree-bob! Now, lemme see," pondered Cigar. "Turn t'other way, 'n put yer heels even with the edge o' the doorway. Now get on yer knees 'n lie right down on yer belly. That's it.

"Now stretch yer right arm as far as she'll go, 'n feel around fer the edge of a board. Yer lookin' fer the end of one of these long floorboards."

71

Frogger stretched himself out but felt only the long, smooth planking that had been used to close over the attic floor when it was built 130 years before.

"Yer a mite shorter than I wuz," suggested Cigar. "I wuz a bit of a string bean when I was yer age. Try crawlin' forward a bit."

Frogger inched along, exploring cautiously with his fingertips, until he felt a break in one of the planks about a foot from the wall. He raised himself to his knees and advanced for a closer look. Sure enough, there was one short, wide board, about the length of a baseball bat, but it wasn't loose enough to pry free with his fingers.

"I think I found it, but it's stuck," Frogger called back over his shoulder.

"Look near the bottom o' that wall. I used ta keep a long nail there ta pry 'er up with," came the reply.

Frogger groped gently around until his fingers tripped over a long, flat spike. He picked it up and slipped its narrow end between the two lengths of floorboard. As he pulled back on the nail, he felt the short board lift briefly before it slipped and fell back into place.

He tried again, this time laying the starship flashlight down so that he could work with both hands. As he lifted the board, he carefully wedged his left thumb under the edge of the plank, holding it there until he could jam the nail down even deeper. It worked. The iron pry caught the bottom edge of the board, and he managed to lever it all the way up until he could grab the end of the plank with both hands. Excited, he heaved it up and exposed the space.

He had just dropped the board to one side and was about to reach into the hole when Cigar shouted.

"Hold on a minute, boy. Don't be touchin' anythin' down there just yet," he warned. Frogger eased around, shining the light in Cigar's face, wondering what had changed his mind.

"I set booby traps ta stop thievin' marauders from gettin' my stuff," Cigar explained. "Go careful. There's a buncha rat traps ready ta spring. Why, they'd snap yer wrist like it wuz a wormy toothpick."

Suddenly, Frogger's enthusiasm for exploration was dampened.

"Well, how am I going to get anything that's down there? Whatever it is."

"We'll find ya a stick or somethin' ta poke around with. It's been 70 years or more since I last had my arm in that hole, but those ol' traps'll still be waitin'."

With that, Frogger sat down, his back to the outside wall, to wait while the twins went off in search of a prod. Outside, the sun must have reached its full height, for midday heat was baking through the roof — he could feel its radiation on top of his head and shoulders. Listening carefully, he heard the gentle murmur of the water passing over Widowmaker Falls and the raucous cawing of a crow. Despite the dust and the darkness, he had to agree that this was a fine hiding place. He wished that it were his.

Brats and Rats

Within a couple of minutes, Kenny appeared at the entrance to the crawl space, a long, black rod clutched in his hand. It was an ebony back-scratcher, a souvenir of a trip the Troths had taken to a resort in the Dominican Republic before the twins were born. The handle was in the shape of a dancing woman with one extraordinarily long arm that reached up to a long-fingered hand, its fingers bent for maximum scratching power. Very weird, thought Frogger, taking it from Kenny.

As he eased back to the hole in the floor, the twins entered the crawl space, anxious to get a full view of their babysitter's exploratory probe.

"I can hold the starship," suggested Kenny.

"So can I," said Kerry.

"No, you can't. It belongs to me. You might break it."

"Wouldn't."

"Too."

Behind them, Cigar settled the argument. "Ya can both sit tight 'n zip yer lips, or we'll stick you in that hole 'n nail the board down. Now give Frogger some room there ta maneuver, 'n listen up in case he needs some real help."

The twins fell silent and turned their attention back to the hole and their babysitter. Frogger had stepped over the opening and was lying down on the far side of it so that he could see Cigar while he worked.

"Set the light right down in the hole so it's shinin' to yer left. The space betwixt the floor joists is about two feet wide 'n goes clear across the attic. I used ta slide my stuff in a ways so's nobody'd see it even if they'da found the loose board."

Doing as he was told, Frogger lowered the light down into the space, then craning his neck, he stuck in his head. Turning slightly sideways and closing his left eye, he squinted down the tunnel-like passage and came face-to-face with a small, fragile-looking white skeleton. He exhaled desperately, determined not to breathe in any of the deceased creature's germs, and yanked his head out of the hole.

"There's something dead down here," he called to Cigar.

"Can we see?" the twins chorused.

"Keep back!" Cigar commanded, correcting himself when he saw Frogger start to retreat from the hole. "No, not you, Frogger. It's prob'ly just an ol' rat or squirrel. How big is it?"

Taking a deep breath, Frogger peeked in for another look.

"It looks pretty long, I guess. It's in a big trap, but it's got no hair or anything. Just bones."

"Well, just pull 'er outta the way with that poker of yers there," Cigar suggested. "Ya might be wantin' it later ta show yer science teacher at school or someone. Lotta folks like skeletons and such."

Frogger pulled the trap clearly into view and then pushed it beyond the opening so that he could get a better look in the secret hiding place.

"What am I looking for, anyway?" he asked, peering beyond the twins, who were fidgeting near the opposite side of the hole.

"Far's I can recall, two or three mean ol' rat traps, an ol' cigar box 'n a big biscuit tin with horses gallopin' round the sides."

With unpleasant visions of more dead rodents, Frogger returned to his task. The starship, whose twin beams were starting to fade, illuminated two dusty shapes in the near distance. Probing carefully along the bottom of the space with the back-scratcher, Frogger made contact with an object buried in dust. Closing his eyes in concentration, he slid the stick farther, caught the edge of what he assumed was another rat trap and pulled it toward him. He opened his eyes to view his catch and was surprised to see an old book. After grabbing it, he shook the dust off and pulled it out of the hole, looking quickly at the cover before passing it to Cigar.

"Oh, ho, I fergot about this," the old man sighed.

"What is it?" Kenny asked.

"Just an ol' scrapbook o' sorts," came the reply. "Nuthin' really. Can ya see the boxes?"

Frogger grunted an affirmative and reached back into the darkness, this time keeping the back-scratcher high so that it would stay clear of the boxes. When his arm was fully extended, he eased it down and felt it touch something. When he tapped it gently, it sounded like the tin box. Catching the far edge of it with

76

the back-scratcher's ebony fingers, he pulled it carefully toward him, feeling the weight of it as it moved. He readjusted his grip as it got closer and raised his head away from the hole for a better look. Somehow, he had managed to fish both the small cigar box and the much larger biscuit tin out at the same time.

Without waiting for an invitation, the twins surged forward and fought for a grip on the smaller of the two. Kenny got it first and lifted up the cigar box, while Kerry slapped at his fingers, until Frogger warned him away.

"Kerry, let Kenny have it. You can get the other one once Kenny gets out of the way."

Triumphant, Kenny wriggled back to a delighted Cigar Davis, who seized the box from him and blew off the dust and cobwebs. What started as a puff turned into a choking cough, as years of fine dust rose into the air around his face.

Frogger brushed off the old biscuit tin with his hands while it was still in the hole, then lifted it up to Kerry, who dutifully passed it back to the old man. Then, turning toward the hole, the youngster volunteered for one last mission.

"Do you want me to crawl down in there to see if there is anything else? I'm not scared."

Behind him, Kenny laughed, but Cigar waved him silent.

"No, that's okay, Kerry," said Frogger. "I'll just feel around one more time with the back-scratcher to see if anything is there, and then we can go."

The little boy headed back into the attic, and Frogger stuck the rod deep into the recess one more time. There was a violent snap, as one of Cigar's booby traps sprang to life, and with

77

a shudder, Frogger felt the peculiar ebony shaft break in two.

"I think we'll just close it up now," he whispered, dropping the dancing-woman handle into the hole. "There's only traps left."

He retrieved Kenny's Space Flight Starship and pulled the piece of planking back into place, listening to Cigar shooing the boys away from his recovered treasures. The old man was refusing to let them examine any of the contents until they were downstairs.

As he emerged from the darkness of the crawl space, Frogger blinked his eyes to get reaccustomed to the light that flooded into the office from the skylights. He had to admit that the room was not as much of a disaster as he had first feared. There were two large pieces of drywall, surrounded by several smaller bits lying near the wall, and a thin layer of plaster dust covered everything, but the air was clear again, and aside from the gaping wounds in the low wall, a thorough vacuuming would probably clear up the worst of the mess.

Cigar Davis caught his look and laughed brightly. "Now don't go gettin' all worried — we'll patch this up later. Right now, I'll just shove this little sofa back in place, 'n no one'll be any the wiser."

Frogger was about to argue the point but never got the chance. Before he could open his mouth, a fire siren began to wail loudly outside. The twins ran to the narrow glass door that led to a small balcony overlooking the driveway and headed excitedly for the stairs.

"There's a fire truck here. I bet the house is on fire," hooted Kenny, as he sent Kerry flying to one side, winning the race to the top of the stairs.

Randy Returns

By the time Frogger caught up to them, the twins were hanging onto the front-porch railing — scared enough of Randy Timmerman to stay close to the house but unwilling to let the big, red fire engine out of their sight.

"Hey, Frogger. I thought the boys there might be interested in checking out one of our trucks. I felt pretty rotten after I scared the little guy so bad, and the chief told me I should pay him a visit."

Kerry looked on dubiously, but Kenny was ready to forgive and forget, especially if it got him closer to the shiny red idling fire truck.

"Come on, Kerry. Maybe he'll give us a ride."

But Kerry was not so easily convinced.

"He's a very scary man," he countered. "I'm afraid of him."

Anxious to mend the rift between the tiny Troth and the fire department, Frogger bent over and put his arm around

Kerry. Kenny had already advanced as far as the bottom of the porch steps and was looking back for encouragement from Frogger to go farther.

"Do you have a chain saw on that rig, Randy?" called Frogger.

"Heck, no," came the answer. "After today, I don't think I'll be allowed to touch one again until I'm an old man."

"See, Kerry, there's nothing there that will hurt you," soothed Frogger. "Randy's really a great guy. He just got carried away this morning. He's trained to save lives, especially kids. I'll go down with you, if you want."

Kerry grabbed Frogger's hand and started down the steps, a signal that Kenny took as permission to rush right up to Randy. By the time Kerry arrived at the truck, Kenny had already been given a helmet to wear and had climbed up onto the shiny chrome running board. Kerry quickly snatched the helmet that Randy offered and retreated a few steps from the grinning firefighter before putting it on. Motioning to Frogger, Kerry indicated that he wanted to climb onto the back of the truck, where there was more equipment to inspect and he would be at a safer distance from Randy.

Wobbling under the weight of the huge helmet, its clear face shield pulled down, Kerry clambered beyond the running board and into a mound of hoses.

"What are these for?" he shouted over the steady throb of the diesel engine.

"Those are the hoses we use to spray water. We hook them onto the side of the pumper here, and then shoot water onto the fire," explained Randy.

Kenny was off the truck and beside him in a flash.

"Can you show us, mister?"

"Sure. If you call me Randy."

Nodding to Frogger, Randy ran a short length of hose off the truck and across the lawn, while Frogger grabbed the opposite end and attached it to the big brass valve on the side of the truck, tightening it with a wrench that was longer than his arm.

"You don't mind if they get a bit wet, do you?" asked Randy. "They look as if they've been rolling in wet chalk anyway. Maybe we can clean them up."

He waved for the twins to join him at the nozzle end and then signaled for Frogger to throw open the valve. He had turned the nozzle to its gentlest spray, and the boys raced through a heavy mist of water to reach him. Opening up the nozzle a bit more, Randy increased the flow pressure and eased his grip slightly as Kenny and Kerry wrapped their arms around the hose. The hose stiffened, lifting the nozzle upward, a motion that raised the twins slightly off the ground. Laughing with the boys, Randy eased off the pressure, let them get their footing back and did it again. This time, the twins fell over onto the ground and lost their grip completely.

Turning back toward them but aiming carefully to one side, Randy soaked the twins with a light spray, daring them to try to approach him. But every time they started toward him, he shot a gentle blast of water against their shins and ankles, knocking them down and sending them rolling across the grass. When he finally shouted for Frogger to turn off the pump and close the valve, the boys had collapsed on their backs in a fit of giggling, thoroughly soaked, the helmets lying some distance away where they had first fallen.

"Hey, you noddle noggins, whatcha doin' down there?" It was Cigar Davis standing on the small attic balcony that was attached to the gable end of the house. He had stepped out of Mrs. Troth's office and had been watching the commotion below for some time.

"Hello up there," yelled Randy. "Are you in trouble? Do you need to be rescued?"

The twins jumped to their feet and ran toward Randy.

"Yes, save him. Save him before he burns to a crisp."

Randy, totally caught up in the sheer pleasure of showing off his equipment and his skills, climbed onto the back of the truck and began to raise the emergency ladder to the little balcony. As he shouted words of comfort to his third-floor victim and urged Frogger and the boys to stand clear of the rig, however, a bright red truck roared into the driveway.

Unfortunately, it wasn't Mrs. Gilmore coming to join in the fun. It was Mrs. Troth in the Red Menace! Her face was a fascinating blend of horror and fear that quickly turned to anger and rage as she spotted first her children, climbing up the sides of the fire truck, and then the wild-haired stranger gleefully waving from her attic balcony. As Randy observed later that evening in the fire-station lounge, she probably would have been happier if her house had been on fire.

Fired!

That night, Frogger sat quietly at the dinner table, pushing his food around on the plate.

"So how was your first day of work?" his mother asked, as she twirled a forkful of spaghetti.

"Not very good," Frogger sighed, managing to avoid eye contact by staring at the base of the wooden salad bowl in the center of the table.

Noting the miserably small portion of food he had taken, Mrs. Archibald assumed that it was worse than "not very good."

"Did the twins give you trouble?" she continued.

"Not really. I mean, they were a handful most of the time, but the trouble was more about me than about them." He paused and then looked to his father, who had grown up in Tichburg. "Do you know a guy named Cigar Davis?"

"Cigar? Everybody knows Cigar Davis. When I was a kid,

83

he was the village's number-one attraction. He and his wife and kids actually lived in this house for years, just down the street from his sister's house — where the Troths live now. His mother was still alive then, but that was a long time ago.

"His two boys were quite a bit older than me, but they just ran wild, until they grew up and moved away. One of them went out West to work on the oil rigs, and I think the other one lives in Florida. If there was an uproar in Tichburg, you could be certain to find Cigar or his kids in the middle of it."

Frogger's mother interrupted her husband's reverie. She had heard hundreds of Mr. Archibald's stories about the characters who lived in the village in the old days. He had left Tichburg himself after high school and had stayed away for 10 years, until he returned to take the newspaper editor's job. He had been 28 years old then and had arrived back with a city-bred wife and a young baby in tow. Over the years, he had told his wife some pretty amazing stories about the Davises — and several of the other families whose descendants still lived in the area.

"How do you know about Cigar Davis?" she asked Frogger.

"Well, he sort of came back to Tichburg today and dropped by the Troths' house for a visit. Mrs. Gilmore had said it was all right. He wanted me to cut his hair, because she was busy getting ready for the fair tomorrow, and while he was there, the house sort of got messed up, and then I had to leave the kids with him to go to Mrs. Gilmore's house, and then Cigar brought the twins over in a wheelbarrow, and the pies burned, and Kerry got his head stuck between the railings on Mrs. Gilmore's porch, and while we were getting it unstuck, Cigar went back to the Troths' house with a sledge-hammer and smashed some holes — including a really big one — in Mrs. Troth's new wall in the attic, and then the fire truck got there, and the kids were playing on it, and . . . well, Mrs. Troth came home early and saw what was going on and the big mess we had made — that I was going to clean up — but she didn't even try to understand. She just fired me and chased Randy Timmerman and Cigar Davis off the property. She said she was going to call the police on all of us. It was pretty awful." Frogger stopped to catch his breath.

His parents sat listening to the story numbly, nodding their heads to signal that they were absorbing all the information, although, in truth, Mr. Archibald was desperately trying to recall whether their household insurance would cover the misdeeds of babysitting offspring. Across from him, Mrs. Archibald was fret-ting silently about the emotional state of the twins and of Sara Troth, whom she had just met. At the time, Mrs. Troth had seemed moody and unsociable, and Frogger's mother doubted whether the day's events would change any of that for the better.

A dismal silence fell across the table, all the Archibalds lost in their own thoughts. Frogger sat looking miserable, worried about what his parents would say next, but a knock at the door brought them quickly back to life.

It was Dunston Troth, looking as if he wished he were somewhere else. He was carrying Frogger's backpack, which he set down on the floor of the hallway as he was ushered into the house.

Mrs. Archibald offered him a cup of tea, but he declined,

apologizing for having interrupted their dinner when they offered him a seat at the table. It was obvious that this visit had not been his idea, and he was struggling over what to say.

"Sara, my wife, wanted me to drop by for a chat about the, ahhh, events of the day."

"Frogger told us that it was not a good day," said Mr. Archibald, hoping to skip over the details he already knew and find out how bad things were going to get between the Archibalds and the Troths. "Let's cut to the chase" was the way he always put it when there were difficult matters to discuss.

"Well, Mr. Archibald . . ."

"Call me James."

"Super. Yes. Absolutely. Well, James, this has probably been the most trying day of our lives. My wife — she's a very sensitive woman — is tremendously upset. She is lying down right now with a terrible migraine headache. When I got home, she asked me to sort things out with you and Frogger. I mean Tad."

Frogger lowered his eyes to the salad bowl, wondering just how much trouble he was in. His stomach was twisting itself inside out, and he was not sure whether he would ever be allowed to babysit again.

"I'm afraid my wife overreacted today. That's not to say there was no damage done, because there was. But most of it has already been cleaned up — except for the rather large hole bashed in the upstairs office. But Sara was quite upset, worried about the boys and the house.

"Well, she called the police and insisted that our home had been invaded and that charges be laid because of the damage done. The officer promised to investigate, but I must admit that I hope nothing comes of it. It seems that this Mr. Davis is well known to the police . . ."

"To everyone, actually," Mr. Archibald added helpfully. "He's sort of a local character. Good-hearted soul, really. Frogger tells us he just got back to Tichburg today. He's been away for a long time."

"In prison?" Mr. Troth queried.

"No. Florida," answered Frogger, assuming that the old man was not a jailbird.

"Well, the details don't really matter at this point, I suppose. Anyway, my feeling is that I am partly at fault for having given so much responsibility to young Frogger, I mean Tad, here. He's not quite 12, after all, and . . ."

"November 11," piped up Frogger.

"I beg your pardon?"

"I'll be 12 on November 11."

"Oh, of course. Well, anyway, I just want you all to know that we will not be holding Tad responsible for any of the damages or missing items and . . ."

"Missing items?" Mrs. Archibald echoed.

"A photographic portrait from our front hall and . . ."

Frogger interrupted, "That was Cigar's. It was a picture of his wife."

"Yes, well, the old man seems to have carried off some smaller items when he left the house, although nothing else appears to be missing."

"Those were his secret treasures, from when he was a kid," explained Frogger. "They were behind the wall upstairs, which is why he smashed those holes. He used to live in your house a long time ago."

"Well, that explains some of the problem, I guess," Mr. Troth concluded. He stood up, signaling his intention to leave. Mr. and Mrs. Archibald rose too, leaving Frogger feeling very small at the far end of the table. Catching a sharp glance from his mother, he stood up as well.

"Needless to say, Sara has asked that Tad be relieved of his babysitting duties. We will take the boys into Amaranth with us to a day-care facility. But we do intend to pay for the six hours that Tad tended the twins."

He reached into his wallet and pulled out three brand-new $10 bills. Mrs. Archibald began to protest, but Dunston Troth raised his hands to silence her.

"If the truth is to be told, Mrs. Archibald . . . "

"Helen," she suggested.

"Helen, yes, super. Well, the boys claim that it was the most fun they've ever had with a babysitter. They're still talking about the fire engine and that wild young firefighter."

"Randy Timmerman," explained Frogger to his parents.

"And they would love to have Tad take care of them again. But maybe when he's a bit older. In a couple of years — without Mr. Davis's help, of course. And don't worry, our insurance will take care of the damages."

He laid the three bills on the table and headed for the door, the Archibalds following close behind him, offering thanks and apologies. Frogger was about to join them, but his pager chirped insistently. Everyone froze in their tracks, waiting for him to answer it. He pushed the RECEIVE button, and Mrs. Gilmore's voice squawked to life.

"Frogger, I'm just down at the fire hall with Cigar and Fred Keeling, from the police detachment. Sounds as if the Troths have their knickers in a knot and plan to visit you and your folks tonight. Might be a good idea to head out to the fair before they get there. Let things cool down a bit. Over."

Dunston Troth's face reddened, as did those of the Archibalds, and he bid them all a hasty good night.

Friday-Night Fireworks

Frogger returned to the table and quickly finished his dinner in silence, then cleared away his dirty dishes and headed to his room. Hauling Peanut from his cage, he stroked the little guinea pig as he sprawled on the floor beside his bed, feeling miserable and somewhat confused.

Logic told him that he should be in serious trouble by now, but everyone seemed to be blaming each other or themselves for all the problems he had caused. He had burned the pies, but Mrs. Gilmore blamed herself. He had let Cigar Davis pound holes in the walls of the Troth house and let Kerry Troth get stuck headfirst in the railings, yet Mr. Troth took the responsibility, even though he had not been there. He had left the Troth kitchen, bathroom and porch in a mess, and while it was safe to say that Mrs. Troth blamed him firmly for that, he recalled her raging attack on Randy Timmerman, in which she had accused the whole fire department of encouraging her boys to climb all over the rig and to play with the hoses.

Randy, in the doghouse for the second time that day, had jumped into the cab of the fire truck and left the Troth yard in such a hurry that he had forgotten to gather up the length of canvas hose on the lawn and had dragged it bouncing all the way up the hill as far as the McAvoy house before stopping to retrieve it. Sensing the potential for a game, Barney the beagle had bounded off the porch and grabbed the hose in his teeth, but the game of tug-of-war ended abruptly when Randy released enough water into the hose to send the dog somersaulting head-over-tail. When Barney had retreated to his porch, Randy quickly rolled up the hose before roaring away.

And now down on the kitchen table lay $30 which Frogger had hardly earned but which he desperately wanted to keep. Not that it was nearly enough to buy himself a decent pair of basketball shoes. At his modest height, he needed every possible advantage if he were to make the all-star team, and a pair of RetroTred Hoopsters seemed the only obvious answer. But he had lost the job that had been going to pay for them, and there were no new sources of big cash in the immediate future. When word got out about this terrible day, Frogger would be the last sitter that anyone called.

By the time his father came up to talk to him an hour later, Frogger was resigned to the fact that his parents would probably ask him to give back the money. But, in fact, Mr. Archibald made no such request. Instead, he sat quietly on the edge of his son's desk, getting the full details of the day's misadventures, asking questions and making observations as he would have if he had been interviewing some local personality for a news story.

Frogger explained how he had apologized a dozen times to Mrs. Troth, trying to convince her to let him back into the house so that he could at least tidy up the kitchen and back porch. But she would have nothing to do with him, and after chasing Cigar Davis out of the house with a flurry of threats and shrieks, she had slammed the door on all of them, hysterically hustling the howling twins away from their dangerous new friends. If she were to be believed, Cigar was on his way to jail, Randy faced imminent expulsion from the fire department and Frogger would never go near her children — or anyone else's — again.

After Randy had escaped the Troths' yard in the fire truck, Frogger and Cigar had started up Riverview Road together until the old man remembered his half-trimmed head. Piling the picture of his wife and his other reclaimed treasures into Frogger's arms, he had stumped quietly back to the house and slipped around to the rear porch to recover the hair clippers. Frogger had hung back in the bushes at the edge of the street until Cigar returned, smiling triumphantly.

"Now, let's get back to yer house 'n finish up that haircut. If I'm gonna be arrested, I wanna look respectable. Though, come ta think of it, a night in jail might solve my accommodation situation quite nicely."

So Frogger had finished trimming the old man's long white hair at his house and then handed over the clippers so that Cigar could tidy up his ragged beard. In half an hour, Cigar had looked less like a crazed Santa Claus and more like the retired farmer that Frogger had assumed he was.

"Oh, Cigar Davis was no farmer when he lived here," corrected Mr. Archibald. "He spent his life dabbling in all sorts of ventures, but I don't recall that he ever farmed.

"For a while, he owned Birdie Pickett's Lucky Dollar store, but he sold it years ago to work at one of the mills down the river. He was in the army for a time during the war and had a little diner once. Used to sell real estate. Did a bit of carpentry. He's been a jack-of-all-trades his whole life and was always working on some scheme to strike it rich. Sometimes, he would leave Tichburg to take a job or start something new, but he always came back.

"His father was quite wealthy. He started the village's first bank at a time when this was a very busy little community. That's how he could afford to build that beautiful big house down by the river, but I'm told that Cigar was not interested in working for his father, and the old man eventually cut him off — refused to have anything more to do with him.

"Cigar was a pretty lovable guy, although it took some people a while to get used to his odd manner. He practically lived on Main Street when I was growing up here. If there were more than four people gathered anywhere, Cigar Davis would be right in the middle of the group, holding court as if he were the mayor or something. Everybody wanted to know what Cigar thought about everything.

"When he was young, folks assumed that he was going to be wildly successful no matter what he did, and by the time they realized that he was just a big, jolly guy with lots of ideas and not a whole lot of ambition, nobody cared. They just liked him for the way he was."

Frogger, still lying on the floor, his feet up on the bed,

asked, "So why did he leave Tichburg?"

His father paused, looking out the window toward the fairground, at the eastern edge of the village. He could see the top of the Ferris wheel poking above some trees and could just hear the faint sound of the music that accompanied the merry-go-round. The Harvest Fair was under way.

"Are you going to the fair tonight?" he asked.

Frogger gave a noncommittal shrug, and his father picked up the story where he'd left off.

"Well, Cigar must have been 70 when he left last time. His wife Hazel had just died, his boys were long gone, of course. I don't think he got along very well with his sister Doris, and I guess he must have decided he still had time for one more adventure. He was living in this house at the time.

"Anyway, he had a great big, old white Cadillac, and a few days after Hazel's funeral, he just loaded it up with whatever he could fit into it and drove off. A few years later, he wrote to Mel Dobbins, the lawyer, and told him to sell the place for as much as he could get and send the money to him in Florida. And now he's back."

"With no money and no place to live," added Frogger sadly. "Because we took his house."

"Bought it," Mr. Archibald corrected him. "At a fair price too. You mustn't worry about Cigar, Frogger. He always seems to land on his feet, and there are lots of old-timers around who like him. Someone will give him a bed until he gets settled."

* * *

Frogger did not go down to the fairground that night. The

94

Harvest Fair was a one-night one-day affair, and he decided to wait until morning. The long, hard day had done much to kill his fair-going spirit, and if Fred Keeling had come out to handle Mrs. Troth's police complaint about him and Cigar, the story would have already spread throughout the community by now.

Fred was a talker, and by the time he had picked up a chocolate bar at Birdie Pickett's Lucky Dollar and stopped for gas and a coffee at Jake Hartington's garage on his way to the fairground, he would have told the story a half-dozen times or more. Frogger was not in the mood to face the questions and comments that a fiasco like this would bring.

It would be bad enough tomorrow, but tonight would be worse. Only the small midway was open on the Friday of the fair, and being stuck in line for the Ferris wheel or the Tilt-O'-Whirl would just make Frogger an easy target. At least on Saturday, there would be plenty of events to divert attention from him, like the horse races and livestock trials as well as all the exhibits and competitions. Besides, he really had no one to go with tonight; he was too old to attend with his parents, even if they were going (which they were not), and in all likelihood, not many kids his age would be there.

He lounged around his room until 10 o'clock, straightening up everything on his bookshelves, lingering over the occasional comic book as he tidied and cleaning Peanut's cage. When he heard the first distant boom of the fireworks, he eased out of his window onto the porch roof, where he watched the red and green and white and gold spidery florets rise and spread, then fall through the navy-blue sky, winking out and leaving gray spirals of smoke in their wake.

Below him, he heard the murmur of his parents' voices as they sat together on the porch steps watching the display and enjoying the cool evening air. Crickets chirped incessantly all around the house, and a small owl hooted in the maple tree beside him. In the background, Frogger could hear the river tumbling over the rocks.

It was a perfect night to be alone on the roof, and he stayed there until the distant fireworks ended with the faint sound of applause and honking horns. A few minutes later, a stream of headlights crept along Main Street as parents drove their children home for the night. Frogger crawled back into his room and climbed into bed without bothering to take off his clothes. The last sound he remembered hearing before he slipped into a restless sleep was the screech of tires and the low bass rumble of the Camaro's stereo as Nicky Knowlton barreled into the driveway next door.

Strangers at the Gate

The next morning, Frogger awoke early, anticipating the fair, and for the first few minutes at least, he was able to push any thought of the Troth babysitting disaster out of his mind.

Although the fair was held in Tichburg, it drew people from miles around. Even families from Amaranth would venture out for a peek at the farm machinery and the animals, oohing and aahing for an hour or two, until they thought they had seen everything there was to see.

But the people around Tichburg didn't really go to the Harvest Fair for the midway or the exhibits or the animals. They went to see each other — and to talk. Sure, the little kids would clamor for rides and beg to eat fudge and french fries and candy floss until they could hardly stand up, but anyone older than 11 was there to visit. In some ways, it was like a huge family reunion; people who had grown up in the area and moved away came back to see their families and spend a day catching up on a year's news. If you were looking for someone in particular, all you had to do was stand by the entrance to the old wooden grandstand and wait. Eventually, everyone would pass by, because the huge roof provided the only shade on the grounds, and the bleachers the only seats.

The old-timers, like Birdie Pickett and Harold Kingsley, the retired postmaster, sat on the lowest levels, helped to their places by a half-dozen volunteer firefighters stationed at the bottom of each set of steps. An unwritten rule decreed that the younger you were, the higher you climbed. The teenagers usually staked out the very top rows, where they could wrestle and hold hands and keep an eye out for their friends, while the younger kids, whose parents had dragged them from the midway or the baseball tournament for a chance to sit in the shade, chased each other up and down the steps and along the full length of the bleachers and generally made a nuisance of themselves until, finally, a parent or an older sibling was dispatched to take them back to the action on the fairground.

Frogger hoped he might see some of his friends who had moved away since kindergarten. Sean Koo had returned to the fair once since he had left Tichburg, but he now lived on the West Coast, and the chances of seeing him again were slim. On the other hand, Casey Oliver, who had moved in grade five, was only a day's drive away, and although he had not yet returned for a visit, he always referred to the fair in his brief letters.

* * *

Frogger leaped out of bed and headed to the bathroom for a quick shower, after which he put on a clean pair of khakis, clipped the pink pager to his belt and pulled on an oversized striped T-shirt to hide it. His parents were still in bed, because it was only 7 o'clock, so he fixed a bowl of stale Fruit Puffies (the only cereal left that didn't contain bran) and a glass of orange juice and quickly gulped down his breakfast.

There was no reason to wait around for his mother and father to get ready. He would ride his bicycle out along the riverside path that served as a shortcut to the fairground and see his parents when they arrived at the fair around mid-morning. This year, he wanted to get there early enough so that he could lend a hand wherever he was needed — and earn a free admission.

The midway was always set up on Friday afternoon by the tough tattooed carnies who traveled all summer from country fair to country fair with their rides and game concessions, but most other things were taken care of early Saturday morning. Doc Timmerman, a successful dairy farmer who had sold his huge herd of Holsteins to his two oldest sons so that he could tend to his magnificent Clydesdale show horses full-time, had been the president of the Tichburg and District Agricultural Committee for almost 10 years and prided himself on getting everything done right on time. Three years in the army as a young man had turned him into a fierce strategist, and 40 years of milking a hundred cows at the crack of dawn each morning had taught him valuable lessons about delegating authority. He ran the fair with an iron fist, and while he was not a popular man, his fairs had always been successful.

By the time Frogger rode up to the main gate, the church committee's pie tent was up, the bingo tables had been assembled behind the grandstand and a crew of teenagers was busily chalking the baseball field. There was still plenty to do, but the 10 o'clock deadline was easily within reach.

Randy Timmerman and three other firefighters were collecting admission ($5 a carload) and directing drivers to the designated parking areas. Cattle trucks were sent to the stock-judging area close to the river, while the horse trailers had to cross the dirt racetrack to the treed end of the infield. Exhibitors from the various equipment dealerships took the shadeless end of the field by the ball diamond, and owners of the classic cars and trucks that were entered in the Queen of the Harvest Parade had to drive halfway around the track so that they would remain out of sight until the procession started. The rest of the early arrivals, most of them women bringing home-baked goods, handicrafts, quilts and their children's art entries, got the choice parking spaces close to the grandstand.

Doc Timmerman was standing tall in the bed of his glistening white 1958 Dodge pickup truck, keeping a watchful eye on things, as he always did. Every firefighter and volunteer crew chief was equipped with one of the fire department's walkie-talkies, and Doc would spend the next two hours barking orders into the microphone of the headset that he wore under his spotless white Stetson cowboy hat. A pair of binoculars hung around his neck, and with his clipped mustache and close-cropped gray hair, he resembled some army general preparing for an invasion. The truck and the Stetson were symbols of Doc's authority at the fairground.

"Johnny, there's a parked horse trailer sticking out halfway across the track. Make sure the fool doesn't intend to

100

leave it there. Over . . . Jake, we need at least a dozen extra bales of straw down in the petting barn. Over . . . Has anyone seen Dolly Gilmore? The craft section is ready for entries, but no one has the key to the shed. Over." There were no pleases or thank-yous, but he was getting things done.

Frogger rolled his bike over to Randy, who greeted him with a hoot.

"Well, I figured we'd be visiting one another in the lock-up last night," said Randy, "the way that Troth woman was carrying on yesterday." The other men chuckled appreciatively, convincing Frogger that Randy's version of the babysitting story had portrayed him in a sympathetic light.

But before he could respond, the choking roar of a badly tuned truck engine caused them all to look up. Behind them, an ancient dump truck approached the gateway, groaned to a halt, sputtered and died. It had been red at one time during its life, and while it was about the same vintage as Doc Timmerman's fabulously restored pickup, it was battered and rusty. A bright blue tarpaulin was tied down over top of the bed of the truck, although one corner of it had blown loose and a rope dangled freely.

A mischievous-looking man wearing a brimless embroidered hat stuck his head out the driver's window and shouted a greeting.

"Good day, fellas. Is your fair open for business?"

The firefighters looked uncomfortably at one another and glanced over at Doc. "He's the man to ask," replied Randy.

Confounded by the sight of the decrepit dump truck, Doc leaned forward across the roof of his pickup, straining to hear the stranger's question. "What's he want?"

The driver swung open his creaking door and jumped to the ground, trotting over to Doc's pickup. Before he spoke, he turned to a young girl about Frogger's age seated high in the passenger seat and waggled his fingers as if to say, "I'll be right back."

"Good day, sir." It was Doc's characteristic colder-than-ice greeting. "What can we do for you?"

"Well, we were just passing by and noticed that you folks are holding a fair today, and we wondered if we might add to the fun?"

"Add to it? How?"

"Well, sir, we're in the sports-shoe business — running shoes and such — and thought that your event would benefit from our latest shoe promotion."

Frogger moved closer to the pickup, while Doc carefully scrutinized the stranger and his truck. Nearly all Tichburgers and area residents who attended the Harvest Fair made a point of washing and polishing their vehicles. It was very clear that this man was not from the area, an assumption borne out by his clothes. He wore a sheepskin vest over a tie-dyed T-shirt. His spindly legs were accentuated by a long, baggy pair of cargo shorts covered with pockets and by a pair of old brown cowboy boots that slapped at his calves when he walked.

"A shoe promotion," repeated Doc, pretending to be thoughtful. "What kind of a shoe promotion?"

"An unmatched-shoe promotion."

Doc stood silent. His walkie-talkie started to squawk, but he turned it off and set it down on the cab.

"I don't understand."

"It's simple, really. Under the tarp, I have — we have — a thousand shoes. Brand-new. Never been worn. Name-brand athletic shoes, and we have chosen Tich . . . ," he stumbled, forgetting the name of the village.

"Tichburg," offered Frogger helpfully. He looked back at the old dump truck and saw the girl slouch lower in her seat.

"Yes, of course. We've chosen Tichburg's summer festival as the site of this year's sale."

"You have a thousand pairs of shoes loose in the back of that truck?" asked Doc.

"Not pairs. Single shoes. Unmatched," explained the man, grinning. "But brand-new out of the warehouse."

"Sounds as if you missed the turnoff for the dump." It was Hap Murray, one of the firefighters with Randy. Hap had a mean streak in him that he often passed off as a sense of humor, turning it against anyone who came within spitting distance. Remembering his bright pink pager, Frogger casually checked to make sure it was still out of sight.

"The dump's back to the north of us," Hap roared, looking to the other men at the entrance for approval. But the shoe man didn't take the bait. He smiled pleasantly at Hap and turned back to Doc, who glowered down from his pickup.

"And what do you intend to do with a thousand shoes in the back of a dump truck?" Doc snapped.

"Well, I know it may sound crazy, but we just dump them in a big pile on the ground and sell them to folks for $5 a shoe." He turned to Frogger and smiled.

Doc mulled over the information. He had dug a toothpick out of his shirt pocket and was chewing on it thoughtfully.

"So people wade into this huge pile of shoes, look for ones that match and buy them?"

"Nope. Won't find any that match," chuckled the stranger. "They may find shoes that almost match, but I guarantee you that no one will come up with a perfect pair. Different colors, different styles, different sizes. Nothing matches."

"Craziest thing I ever heard," muttered Hap, but Doc continued to stand upright, watching the growing line of trucks and cars backed up behind the shoe truck.

"Doesn't seem like folks would be interested," he finally announced. Then, looking down at Frogger, he asked, "What do you think?"

Kitchen 'N Craft Shed

Frogger was stunned. Doc Timmerman did not speak to kids, certainly never to ask for their opinion, and here he was wanting Frogger's thoughts on a truckload of mismatched shoes.

"You're James Archibald's boy, aren't you?" demanded Doc.

"Yes, sir."

"He's a good man, always gives us a nice write-up in the paper. I knew your grandfather when he was alive too. Had a good eye for horses. So what do you think about these shoes? Should we send the man on his way? Doesn't make much sense to me."

Hap was behind him, nodding like a fool, but Frogger hesitated. "Are there any RetroTreds? The gel-filled ones for basketball?"

The stranger beamed happily, sensing in Frogger an ally. "You mean Hoopsters. Must be at least 20 in there." He called back to the girl in the cab. "Bug, how many RetroTred

Hoopsters we got in that batch? . . . 20? . . . 30?"

The girl named Bug shrugged. "Yeah, at least 30. What size are you?"

"About a seven."

"Oh, yeah. We'll have something that fits you." The shoe man looked back up at Doc. "Or at least ONE that will fit him."

Hap sensed that the tide was turning and joined in on the joke being made at Frogger's expense.

Doc looked back down. "So, son, you're prepared to wade through a pile of shoes looking for something that might fit?"

"Sure. I guess. There'll probably be other people interested too. Mr. Bartlett likely could use two or three shoes." Ken Bartlett, a retired barber with bad circulation, had lost a foot earlier that year. "Right now, he has to buy two shoes and throw one away. And Mrs. Gilmore was saying that her Aunt Loris has really swollen feet that are different sizes and has stopped wearing shoes altogether. And . . ."

Doc waved for him to stop. "Well, I guess there's no harm in letting you in," he said to the shoe man. "Pay the boys down there the $50 vendor's fee and set up over next to the hog-feed display, at the end of the infield."

He picked up his walkie-talkie, clicked it on, turned his back and started issuing orders, leaving the little man to hurry back to his truck. Waving to Randy, he promised that he would pay on the way out and coaxed the truck engine to life. As they pulled through the gate, Frogger tried to get a better look at the girl, but she had just about shrunk out of sight. The old truck bounced down onto the racetrack, its horn hooting happily, and Frogger got back on his bike and rode

106

over to the Kitchen 'N Craft Shed to find Mrs. Gilmore.

* * *

He found the fire chief hovering over a display of baked goods — pies, cakes, cookies and bread — arranging them carefully into the categories in which they would be judged. Another half-dozen women were doing similar tasks with quilts and stuffed toys and knitted sweaters and any other craft that adults or children could make at home with their own hands.

"There you are, Frogger. I've been waiting for you to get here. We need a hand to hang up some of the really big quilts on the wall there. Doc sent us over some nails and wire and a hammer, but he surely can't expect us to climb up on those wobbly tables and start hammering away."

Mrs. Gilmore did not get along with Doc Timmerman at moments like these. She suspected that he resented having a woman for a fire chief, and he seemed to go out of his way to prove that she could not do simple jobs as well as a man. But in view of her age and stature, she was not about to start climbing on furniture to prove a point. She cleared a path on the table of sewing projects for Frogger to walk along and gave him specific instructions about where to hammer each nail. Working quickly and carefully, he managed to anchor a dozen nails into the wall and string the wire from nail to nail. With that done, two women started to hand him the quilts that were to be hung, while Mrs. Gilmore stood back to offer suggestions about how to position them.

By the time he was finished 20 minutes later, the shed had been transformed into a bustling gallery of handicrafts, preserves and baked goods. There was a steady stream of entrants, each bearing something for competition, mostly older women accompanied by their husbands or grandchildren. At the far end of the wall, dozens of paintings by the students of Tichburg Public School were on display, and Frogger wandered over to see who had entered. On the way, he passed macraméd toilet-paper covers, crocheted toilet-seat warmers, tea cozies, tissue-box holders, doilies and even a knitted ballerina holding a roll of paper towels above her head.

Most of the kids' paintings had been done for the school's spring Earth Day poster contest, their creators hoping to win some prize money from the Harvest Fair committee without having to do any new work. On tables below the art, there were a dozen other craft categories represented: sewing, knitting, papier-mâché, modeling clay, and so on, with maybe three or four entries in each. But on closer inspection, Frogger noticed that almost half of all these entries had been submitted by Katie Timmerman, a scheming 10-year-old who happened to be Doc Timmerman's granddaughter. Perhaps to please her grandparents, but more likely to skim off the prize money, she had entered at least one item in all 12 categories. At $5 for each first prize and $2 for each second, she was sure to win at least $30. Frogger was disgusted — but more by the perpetrator than the scheme. He never would have stooped so low, but he had to admit that it would be a nice profit for a day's worth of halfhearted work.

When he looked up, Frogger spotted Mrs. Gilmore waving to him. She had another job for him, replacing a dozen dead bulbs in the string of lights that hung across the top of the center-aisle table of pickles, jams and preserves.

As he carefully climbed up a rickety ladder that someone had found, Mrs. Gilmore chatted amiably about her burnt pies.

"I must admit, I was a bit upset yesterday about those pies — although I tried not to show it. But then I got to thinking about how it really was time to let someone else win the meringues for a change. After all, I've won that category for the past seven years.

"But, you know, I hated to waste those pies. Every other year, I send them over to Mrs. Codger's retirement home, but I couldn't do that with burnt meringue, even though they would taste perfectly all right. So I talked to Doc Timmerman's wife last night, and we decided to use them for the first annual Tichburg pie-eating contest. I've cut them into quarters, so there's enough for 16 entrants."

Frogger looked down on his beaming friend, delighted that she had found a use for the pies, although he had hoped that one of them would have made its way to his house.

"And just to get the young people interested in entering the contest, I put your name at the top of the sign-up sheet on the side of the grandstand. It starts at 10:45."

Great, thought Frogger, not only did he burn the pies, but he was going to have to eat part of one of them in front of 600 people. He grinned his thanks at Mrs. Gilmore and returned to his lightbulb duties. He had never even seen a pie-eating contest before, but he could imagine how it was done — no forks, no hands, no napkins. Just drop your face in and chew. Frogger was getting a bit old for that sort of nonsense, but if it kept Mrs. Gilmore happy and took the pain out of her

109

scorched meringues, he would do it.

By the time he was done, she had disappeared. The Kitchen 'N Craft Shed was completed for another year, and Mrs. Gilmore had headed back home to man the fire phone.

New Kid in Town

Frogger recovered his bike from the shed wall, right where he had left it, and rode over toward the Vegetable Patch, beside the cattle pens. No one bothered to lock up much of anything around Tichburg — certainly not bicycles. During the fair, some people were a bit suspicious of the rough-looking characters who worked the midway, but the truth was that they were far too busy collecting money from the fairgoers at the rides, food concessions and games to bother stealing anything like a bicycle.

Frogger had noticed that the city families usually locked their cars up tight when they parked — carefully closing their windows and tucking their valuables (like music tapes and children's toys) out of sight, just to be safe. But hardly anybody else bothered. Some of the old-timers even left their keys in the ignition, but Mr. Archibald claimed that they were living in a dreamworld if they thought people were still that

111

honest. The problem with locking a car at the fair was that the sun got so hot and beat down on the metal roofs so relentlessly, everything melted inside when you climbed back in: chocolate bars, crayons and kids.

A few years back, Nicky Knowlton and two of his friends had been caught rifling through the unlocked cars in the shady infield area, but they had been looking for cigarettes and loose change, not anything expensive. Doc Timmerman, spotting them with his binoculars from the back of his white Dodge, had sent in a squad of parking attendants, who caught the trio red-handed. Doc then made the three boys climb into the back of his truck and, with his son Randy riding shotgun, drove them several miles north of the village and dropped them off in the middle of nowhere. He warned them not to even think about hitchhiking, and by the time they had trudged back to Tichburg, it was dark and the fair was long over.

Not much was happening at the Vegetable Patch. Most of the entries had already arrived. Two men from Tyler's Seed and Feed Mill had a big, old weigh scale so that people entering giant pumpkins in the contest could ease them off their pickup trucks and onto the scale before rolling them into the display line.

Harriet Brimley and her nephew were helping the judges work their entry into position when Frogger wheeled up, but he stayed back, aware of the fact that an out-of-control giant squash could crush everything in its path. This one was as high as Frogger's chest and seemed headed toward the 400-pound mark. It would probably win, but everyone knew that the really big pumpkins were left in the fields, where they could reach 600 pounds or more by Hallowe'en. Those were the real champions, and the growers at Tichburg's Vegetable Patch were just entering their second-string pumpkins, which had no chance for the serious prize money that could be won at the National Farm Show in November.

Tired of watching them struggle with their unstable load, Frogger rode past the livestock stalls, where the local farm kids were busy giving their calves and lambs a final brushing. Tissy Grant, his weekend babysitter from three years ago, was struggling to braid flowers through the halter on her Jersey cow and stopped to wave at Frogger, which was a mistake, because the animal swung its head back and snatched a mouthful of daisies out of her hand. She laughed about it, though, and gave her shoulders an exaggerated shrug.

He would come back later to visit, but for now, he was headed for the open half-mile track. After the Queen of the Harvest Parade, there would be horse races throughout the day, and no bicycles or pedestrians would be allowed on the track, but right now, it was free for the taking. It was almost 9:30, and the grounds were becoming more crowded. Frogger weaved carefully around people, saying hi and nodding to neighbors and a couple of his teachers as he moved clockwise around the track — toward the classic cars and trucks lined up waiting for the parade. At 10 o'clock, Doc Timmerman would drive to the head of the line in the company of the unbearable Holly Byford, this year's Queen of the Harvest, and lead the collection of old Model T's, antique pickups and tractors, a couple of low-rise hot rods and a vintage fire truck that was of no practical use other than to be driven in parades. Once the

113

vehicles had completed their circuit, the horses would take over the track, the midway would come to life and the competitions would begin in earnest.

Delegations of noteworthy citizens would circulate through the Kitchen 'N Craft Shed tasting pies and cakes, while government agriculture reps and a couple of farm-association directors would judge the 4-H Club livestock and the garden vegetables. As a newspaperman and a respected member of the community, Frogger's father had been asked many times to be a baked-goods judge but had always refused, for fear of upsetting too many of his subscribers. He claimed that it was easier and cheaper simply to buy several plates of pie at the church ladies' tent and compliment each one than it would be to choose six or seven winners and create dozens of losers.

As Frogger tore along the track, Barney, the McAvoys' beagle, ran in front of him chasing a terrified rabbit which had only recently realized that its home had been taken over by hundreds of fairgoers. Frogger swerved to miss the dog, but his skidding back wheel caught the edge of a ripe cow pie deposited by one of the 4-H heifers, and the bicycle slid out from under him, sending him sprawling toward the inside edge of the track.

He rolled once, missing another cow pie, and jumped to his feet, hoping that no one had noticed his spill, but on bending over to pick up his bike, he heard a voice calling to him.

"Hey, you . . . what's-yer-name."

Frogger looked up and recognized the girl from the dump truck, not so much because he remembered what she looked like but because she was sitting on top of a huge pile of running shoes. She was about 50 feet away, but it was clear that she remembered him. She was waving or pointing, so he picked up his bicycle, checked quickly for damage and walked toward her.

"Frogger," he called.

"What?"

"My name's Frogger. You asked what my name was."

She gave him a sour look. "I did not."

She was taller than he was, wearing jeans and a T-shirt, with a bandanna wrapped around her head. He couldn't tell whether she was being mean or just teasing.

"You yelled, 'What's your name?' and I told you Frogger," he explained.

"No. I called you 'what's-yer-name' because I didn't know what it was. Frogger? What kind of name is that, anyway?" She had switched from being sort of mean to sort of curious.

"Just a name. So what did you want?"

"Your parents named you Frogger?"

"No, it's a nickname. What did you want me for?"

"Frogger is a really weird name."

"Well, people around here got used to it, and it sure beats Thaddeus." As soon as he had uttered his real name, he suspected that he would quickly regret it, but the girl did not burst out laughing — yet.

"Umm, I guess that's why Frogger sounds so . . . acceptable," she mused.

"So what's your name?"

"You dropped something."

"What kind of name is . . . I mean, what?"

"You dropped something over there when you dumped your

115

bike." She strode over to the track, spotted the cow dung and made a face, skirting around it to get to his pager. It was lying there in the dirt — looking very pink in the bright sunlight.

"Ewwwhh." She made a preposterous grimace as she picked it up. "What on earth is this?"

He reached for it, but she pulled it back to have a closer look. "Don't tell me, it's a Barbie walkie-talkie."

"It's a pager. I'm a firefighter, and that's my pager."

"Firefighter? A midget firefighter? This is really weird. When we pulled off the highway into this place, I told my dad that it felt totally weird, but this is too much. Are your fire trucks pink too?"

"No. Red and yellow." He caught his error as soon as the words left his mouth, but it was already too late.

"Like red with yellow stripes or yellow with red polka dots?" Her curiosity was leaning back toward meanness.

"No, three are red, and one is yellow. We just bought the yellow one used from the national airport. It's a pumper with a hydraulic ladder."

"You really are a firefighter? How old are you?"

"Twelve. Almost. And I'm sort of a special assistant to the fire chief, Mrs. Gilmore. When she needs help, she calls me on the pager."

"A woman fire chief. That's cool. So she's just really into pink, huh?"

"No, it was the only color left at the ElectroMart. I'm probably getting a new one next week." He sensed her curiosity returning. "What's your name?"

"So what kind of calls do you get?"

116

Remembering the burnt pie meringues, Frogger thought carefully. "Well, yesterday, for instance, there was some danger of a fire due to a suspected hot spot in a kitchen. But the rest of the crews were busy, so they called me in to keep an eye on it. So what's your name?"

"Neat. Did it end up catching fire?"

"Almost. I got to it in time. The chief was pretty happy I was around."

He reached for the pager, and she handed it over, giving it a playful tug as he started to take it.

"So what's your name?" Frogger was determined to learn her name, but his question was interrupted.

"Bug! Bug! Over here." It was her father, waving merrily as he dogtrotted across the dusty track, stepping gingerly around the fresh obstacles that dotted the ground.

"Bug?" asked Frogger. "You were making fun of me, and your name is . . ."

"Bug. I mooched some cardboard and a marker to make a sign, but your handwriting is probably better than mine."

Bug started to walk back to the shoe pile, and Frogger followed, clipping the pager back onto his belt and pulling his shirt over top of it. Bug looked unhappy again as her father discussed their options.

"What about 'Loose Tongues, Lonely Soles: $5 each'?"

"No one will know what that means," his daughter argued. "Why don't we just write 'Shoes $5 Each. See Shoe-Girl Freak for Details'? "

"Bug, don't be like that. This is going to be great. Hey, wait a minute, I remember you." He had turned to Frogger

117

and reached out enthusiastically to shake his hand.

"Man, I thought we were toast until you spoke up. You were great — quick thinking. Coming up with those names of people who would want single shoes."

"It wasn't fast thinking, really," shrugged Frogger. "Just the truth. Single shoes make a lot of sense."

"Welcome to Tichville," said Bug sarcastically, "home of the One-Shoe Wonders."

"Bug, back off. This kid, what's your name, son? He's a valuable acquaintance."

"Don't tell him your name. We'll be here for hours."

"Frogger, sir," said Frogger quietly. "My real name is Thaddeus, and they used to call me Tad, until I got to kinder-garten, then they called me Tadpole, and when I grew older, they called me Frogger."

"Oh, brother," moaned Bug.

"That is truly fascinating, Frogger. Did Bug tell you how she got her name?"

"Father . . ."

"It's really quite simple. She was a pest. Always buzzing around like an insect, but we couldn't call her mosquito or horsefly, and pest seemed too rude, so somehow we settled on Bug. Actually, she's more of a pest now. Back then, she was just as cute as a bug."

"Don't you have a fire to put out or something?" Bug asked Frogger as she glared at her father.

"Well, there's a pie-eating contest that starts right after the parade, and I promised to go in it."

"You're kidding. A pie-eating contest? Will there be a

118

seed-spitting competition after that? Maybe a greased-hog rassling match. Oh, man, get me out of here."

"Bug, stop that right now." Her father's good humor had evaporated. "We owe Frogger here a favor. His good work has brought us a chance at a grubstake, and I intend to reward it." He lifted up an old cardboard box to reveal two RetroTred Hoopsters. One was green, the other red.

"Go ahead. Try them on."

Frogger dropped to the ground, tore off his old worn sneakers and slipped on the RetroTreds. Sure, they were different colors, but they were size seven and felt wonderfully comfortable. He jumped up, faked a shot with an imaginary basketball, landed low and made a sharp right twist, pretending to dribble.

"Wow, these are fantastic. They must be worth $100. Thanks. I don't know how to thank you. You're really kind."

"They're actually worth $115 at Athlete's Heel stores," said Bug's dad.

"Well, great. I really appreciate this." He crammed his old shoes into his backpack and bent over to pick up his bike, but the shoe man touched him gently on the shoulder.

"Aren't you forgetting something, son?"

"I am?"

Bug rolled her eyes, giving her father a disgusted look.

"He means you owe him $10 — $5 a shoe."

Tichburg on Parade

Frogger was elated with his RetroTreds. They were so light, they made him feel as if he could defy gravity with every step. The bladders of gel in the soles and sides gave him new powers of movement — it felt as though he could walk on air, travel great distances effortlessly. When basketball tryouts opened next month, he would be able to run back and forth on the court forever, scoring endless baskets. These shoes would turn him into an invincible basketball machine.

He mounted his bike and turned back to wave to Bug's father, but neither of the shoe-sales duo was paying any attention to him. Bug was bent over the blank piece of cardboard as her father hovered above her, making literary suggestions that she seemed to be ignoring.

Invigorated by his new shoes, Frogger headed for the track, but just as his front wheel hit the dirt, a fire siren sounded. It was the signal for the parade to begin. Realizing that it was too late to make a circuit of the track now, Frogger dismounted and leaned his bike up against the clapboard wall of a nearby rest room. He would have to delay his ride until the end of the day, when the horse races were finished.

Settling back against the wall, he noticed a familiar figure waving energetically to him. It was Cigar Davis, straw fedora in hand, beckoning him over. The parade was just coming around the far curve, so Frogger scampered across the dusty track to join the old man.

"Frogger, my son. Glad ta see yer still a free man. I thought ya'd be confined ta quarters fer a year after our little adventure." He was bubbling over with energy. "Ahhh, but ya did a great thing helpin' me fetch my little mementos."

Frogger nodded quietly, smiling.

"So wuz that Troth woman mad or what? Oh, the words that came outta her mouth. Talks like a lawyer. Threaten this, damages that. Trespass. Invasion. I only wanted what wuz rightfully mine, 'n there was hardly any trouble caused. I mean, it wuz my family home, fer tarnation's sake."

Cigar took a breath and laughed. He held a coffee in one hand, and with the other, he slipped his hat back on his well-shorn head.

"Well, that wuz a fine haircut you gave me last night. I wuz lookin' nigh on respectable by the time the police made it out ta the fire hall ta talk my ear off. That cop Keeling had a lot ta say, but I guess he wuz just doin' his job. In the end, he took a right hard look at me 'n knew I meant no harm, so he said there'd be no charges so long as I made restitution. Restitution. Ha! 'Do I look rich?' That's what I sez ta him.

121

Why, I could fix the whole shebang myself in a coupla hours."

Frogger decided that there was no sense arguing with Cigar about the wisdom of a return visit to the Troth house.

"So when he wuz done with me, Dolly Gilmore came by ta take her turn. She tore a strip offa me 'n that young Randy Timmerman like we wuz village idiots run amuck. I mean, it wuz clear ta me why certain things went wrong yesterday, but she'd have none of it. Ahhh, well. In the end, she settled down 'n invited me back ta the house fer a bite o' supper."

He paused for a sip of coffee and smiled as he swallowed it down, savoring the taste.

"Ya know, I think that woman's got a tender spot fer me. She offered me a room at her house 'til I get settled. She's really kinda sweet — took good care of my Hazel when she wuz so sick at the end. But it's just so doggone hard ta stay on her good side. It's a wonder she wuz ever married. She sets a mighty high standard fer herself 'n expects the rest o' us ta measure up."

Frogger was relieved to hear that his new friend would not be sleeping on the street and was about to say as much when he remembered the treasures he had hauled out of the crawl space. So much had happened since then, he had almost forgotten about the two boxes and the scrapbook.

At the risk of sounding too nosy, Frogger casually asked, "Did you get all your stuff sorted out at Mrs. Gilmore's last night? You know, your old boxes and stuff?"

"Yep, thank ya."

"Was everything still there, just like you left it?"

"Oh, indeedy. Plenty o' things I fergot too."

122

Frogger couldn't stand it any longer and blurted, "So what was all that stuff?"

Cigar's posture stiffened slightly, and he turned slowly to face the boy.

"Lotsa memories, son. And a few secrets." And then, looking kindly at Frogger, he relaxed his shoulders and said, "It's a long story, but I reckon you've earned the right ta hear it . . ."

But before the old man could continue, the parade started down the home stretch of track that would take it in front of the grandstand, and talk of his boyhood treasures came to an abrupt halt. For the next 10 minutes, Cigar switched into announcer mode, describing every vehicle and horse team that moved past. Despite his long absence from Tichburg, he still seemed to know most of the people, and he even claimed to have once owned a couple of the fully restored old cars that drove by.

* * *

When the procession had passed, Doc Timmerman executed a U-turn at the end of the track's straightaway and doubled back to give the grandstand crowd a chance to show their appreciation for his organizational talents with a large round of applause. His white Dodge glided to a stop in front of the bleachers, and he gallantly bounced from the cab to hold the door open for the smiling Harvest Queen. As Holly Byford offered a cheesy grin that was 90 percent teeth and 10 percent lips, she took Doc's arm and did a little curtsy. Doc, meanwhile, removed his Stetson and waved it to the throng. There were cheers and applause and calls of "Good job, Doc" from the crowd as the pair advanced to the grandstand itself to take their places of honor for the first competition. Down on the track, Randy Timmerman trotted over to the idling Dodge, jumped into the cab and prepared to shuttle it back to the parking area for his father. But aware that almost every eye in Tichburg was on him, he could not resist the chance to show off.

Revving the engine, he popped the clutch and cranked a sharp left turn. The rear end of the Dodge swung quickly around as Randy executed a perfect donut in the middle of the dirt track. He waved playfully to the crowd as he rocketed past in a cloud of dust, and the audience responded with a roar, laughing, hollering and clapping, in a display that was arguably equal to the ovation that Doc and the Harvest Queen had just received.

For his part, the president of the Tichburg and District Agricultural Committee forced a smile through clenched teeth, muttering to the beaming Holly Byford, "It's time that boy grew up."

But Holly had missed Randy's stunt completely and assumed that this second burst of applause was to mark the occasion of the Harvest Queen's having just taken her seat. She regally stood and turned to face the crowd, offering another royal wave and marveling at the hometown's enthusiasm for their Queen.

Pigs and Pies

A fenced-in scrubby patch of grass about the size of a hockey rink lay between the track and the grandstand, and it was here that the main competitions would take place. Throughout the morning, both babies and farm animals would be judged for their looks and deportment. Logs would be sawed and large spikes pounded into huge blocks of wood in races against the clock. Various rival teams would have tugs-of-war against each other until a new fair champion had been declared. Square dancers would reel around on a small plywood stage, followed by stepdancers, fiddlers and, in recognition of modern trends, gymnasts. But before anything else started, there was to be the first annual pie-eating contest, which promised to be the messiest event of the day.

When Frogger mentioned the event to Cigar, the old man was ready to sign up for it himself, until Frogger explained that the contestants had to be under 12 years of age. Accepting the news in good spirit, Cigar immediately took on the task of coaching his young friend instead.

"Now, a pie-eatin' contest is no time ta be actin' prissy," he advised. "I've watched plenty o' these things in my time 'n been in more'n I can remember. It's been my observation that them that lose are the ones that're scared o' gettin' a bit messy. Normally, I'd recommend a haircut before a show-down like this, but yer hair's not too bad. The ones with long hair, 'specially girls, end up with a hunk o' hair in every bite. Course, that's to yer advantage, cuz it slows 'em down somethin' awful."

Frogger nodded dutifully, looking around to size up the competition. He noticed a knot of younger kids from his school and wondered what the lower age limit was. He began to fear that he would be competing against a bunch of 6-year-olds.

Meanwhile, Cigar continued.

"The real trick ta winnin' is ta use yer chin or forehead 'n smash the pie into small pieces so's you can just suck 'em up 'n chew 'em down fast. The others'll be droppin' their faces down into the pie, but all they'll get is filling 'n a snootful of meringue. The crust'll still be on the plate. They may eventually finish, but the smashers'll be pickin' pie outta their teeth long before that."

Looking past Cigar, Frogger spotted the Troth family approaching them, and for a moment, he worried that Mrs. Troth was coming back to yell some more. But when she caught sight of Frogger and Cigar, she ground to a sudden halt, gathered the twins around her and changed direction. At first, her husband had seemed confused, but when he spotted

Frogger and Cigar, his baffled look turned into a sheepish grin. Pushed along with the twins, Mr. Troth was being herded toward the nearest aisle that led up into the grandstand. Not realizing that the lower tiers were unofficially reserved for the senior citizens of Tichburg, the Troths stumbled their way along the second row, tripping over walkers and canes until they found four empty spaces. They sat surrounded by the residents of Mrs. Codger's retirement home, affectionately known as Codger's Lodgers, who were there hoping to win the prize for the oldest fairgoer.

"Nostril blockage is another problem," warned Cigar, oblivious to the Troths' arrival. "If ya get any fillin' up yer nose, you've lost fer sure. If ya try ta fight it, you'll end up inhalin' the whole darn chunk of pie right into yer lungs, 'n you'll choke ta death on the spot — just rollin' 'n coughin' 'til ya croak in front of all them people. Why, ya'd ruin the day fer everyone."

* * *

Mercifully, the pie-eating contest was short. Very short. The 16 contestants — 4 girls and 12 boys, ranging in age from 8 to 11 — were required to kneel down on the ground beside a length of heavy plastic sheeting, facing the grandstand. The contestants each had a quarter of one of Mrs. Gilmore's scorched lemon meringue pies in front of them, and at the sound of a starter's pistol, they were to start eating — keeping their hands behind their backs.

As he knelt down, Frogger could feel hundreds of pairs of eyes on him. He was not a shy boy normally, but appearing before so many people, even though he knew most of them, was very difficult for him. He thought of Cigar's warning about choking to death in front of such a huge crowd and grew even more nervous.

Above the low buzz of the crowd, he heard two shrill little voices calling out his name. It was the Troth twins cheering for him.

"Come on, Frogger! You can do it! Go, go, go, Frogger!"

They continued for almost half a minute, until their mother finally shushed them.

Crack. The pie race began, and Frogger focused on the task at hand. Some of the contestants ate daintily, nibbling like polite dinner guests on the crust first, while others shoved their faces in deep, covering their eyes and ears with meringue and lemon filling. But Frogger had learned the key to success from Cigar and led with his chin. With three or four sharp jabs, he shattered the crust that had won Mrs. Gilmore so many ribbons at past fairs and proceeded to wolf down the broken pieces, alternately sucking and chewing until the aluminum pie plate was empty. He kept his nose high and didn't bother looking around at his competitors. No time wasted — and no nostril blockage.

Nine seconds after the start, Frogger Archibald leaped to his feet, bouncing up and down in his red and green RetroTred Hoopsters, punching the air wildly as if he had just sunk the winning point in the season's final championship basketball game. He had never before been so animated, so excited, so energized. Riding the rush of adrenaline that sweeps through all top athletes at the climax of a game, Frogger was experiencing the sweet taste of victory.

128

While Frogger was pumped over his win, he was not nearly as pumped as the three squealing pigs that Nicky Knowlton had turned loose. Freed from the confinement of the pens beside the grandstand, the trio of porkers came running hard around the corner, sending bystanders, young and old, scurrying in all directions. And as every farmer in that audience knew, a running pig is an unstoppable force, not just because of its speed but also because it is low to the ground and has better balance than its short legs and little trotters should allow. Indeed, if it had not been for the pies, those three little pigs might have kept running for the rest of the day, but instead, they barreled toward the row of 15 partially eaten pie slices, snorting and grunting their delight at their good fortune.

The contestants fled the scene, abandoning their plates to the pigs, who made even shorter work of the pie than Frogger had. As Randy Timmerman later noted, Frogger could eat pie fast, but even he would need a head start to beat a pig.

Fast-Break Frogger

With the arrival of the pigs, Frogger was forced to cut his victory dance short. Pandemonium erupted as children and organizers fled to the safety of the grandstand steps, while parents and pig farmers headed down the same steps to rescue their children and animals. The commotion had attracted the attention of people on the midway, and the entrance to the grandstand was soon jammed by people trying to get in bumping up against the flow of those trying to get out. Realizing that it would be a long wait before he could get his ribbon and the envelope with his $5 in prize money, Frogger decided that this might be a good time to get cleaned up. He could come back later for his prize, when things had quieted down.

Besides, he had not yet seen his parents, and it was well past their agreed-upon meeting time. They would want to treat him to a few rides and some midway food, and he didn't intend to rob them of that pleasure. After a minute's search through the crowd, he spotted his backpack and got to it just ahead of one of the frenzied pigs. Then, glancing at the massive crowd trying to squeeze through the exit, Frogger headed to the long, low chain-link fence and vaulted over it easily, once again marveling at the luxurious power that his new shoes gave him.

The rest room, where he had left his bike, was across the track, and he hoped that he could get to it without Bug or her father seeing him. He wanted to pay them another visit, but he didn't want to do it while his face was coated with meringue and lemon pie filling. As he approached the track, he heard Doc Timmerman on the public-address system announcing the first race of the day.

"Stand clear of the track. Everyone stay off the track."

Those crossing the track moved quickly along, and a few seconds later, the announcer's voice drawled: "They'rrrre offfff."

The thunder of hooves approached, and everyone craned forward to watch the first of the day's eight harness races. His grandfather, a passionate race fan, had taken Frogger to these races since the age of 2. They had loved to stand close to the track to feel the pounding of the hooves and to hear the calls of the drivers.

Dressed in brightly colored silk shirts and matching helmets, their eyes encased in protective goggles, the drivers flicked their whips over the horses' ears, urging them on faster and faster. The drivers rode large-wheeled carts called sulkies, and Frogger sometimes liked to imagine that they were Roman charioteers from centuries ago, wildly racing each other to the finish line.

He was so intent on watching the horses that he didn't

131

notice the entire Troth family had come up beside him. Indeed, if Mrs. Troth had known that she was drifting toward Frogger, she would have headed in a different direction. But once the twins had spotted their former babysitter, it was too late to take evasive action.

"Look, it's Frogger!" shouted Kerry.

"I saw him first," argued Kenny, pushing his brother to one side and grabbing hold of Frogger's shirt.

"Hey, you're covered in yellow slime."

"We saw you win the contest."

"You eat like a pig."

The boys looked up at Frogger, then glanced at each other and started to giggle.

Frogger turned his gaze away from the horses long enough to smile at them, while avoiding their mother's eyes. She, in turn, was trying frantically to find an escape out of this uncomfortable situation. Seven horses thundered by. Assuming that all the horses had passed and seeing an opportunity to get away, Mrs. Troth grabbed the boys and stepped out onto the track. But what she didn't know was that an eighth racer had broken stride and fallen behind the rest of the pack. In her haste to avoid contact with Frogger, she headed directly into the path of the oncoming horse.

Frogger saw the impending disaster out of the corner of his eye and lunged forward with flailing hands. Mrs. Troth was one step ahead of him and had still not noticed the horse, although she did sense Frogger's pursuit. Speeding up, she was almost at a run when a panicky shout from her husband caused her and the twins to look up. Kenny and Kerry broke free of their mother's hands and darted back to safety at the edge of the track. The last thing Mrs. Troth saw before she fainted dead away was the terrified eye and foaming mouth of the horse that was bearing down on her, half a pace away.

Taking full advantage of his momentum and the gravity-defying power of his new RetroTreds, Frogger bounced forward, launching himself into the air as if to take a pass under the net. But instead of grabbing a basketball, he grabbed Mrs. Troth by both shoulders and somehow managed to pull her out of harm's way with a tackle that would have earned him a penalty and probably a trip to the showers if it had happened on the basketball court. But it had happened at the Tichburg fairground in front of hundreds of spectators, and instead of a penalty, Frogger received the adoration of an entire village.

After he landed, hunched like a cat that was ready to spring again, Frogger could not bear to turn and see whether Mrs. Troth had been trampled by the horse and sulky. Instead, he rose slowly with his back to her prone body, which was lying still in the dust. The adrenaline that had come to his aid mere seconds before now threatened to overwhelm his body — he felt a wave of nausea, and his knees began to shake uncontrollably.

* * *

When Mrs. Troth opened her eyes a minute or two later, she looked up and saw the silhouettes of a dozen figures peering down at her. They pressed forward in a circle, offering suggestions and comfort.

"Don't move."

"You had better get up."

"Are you hurt?"

"Don't worry, you'll be fine. You just passed out."

"What were you doing on the track in the middle of a race?"

"What's her name? Who is she?"

"I think she's that antique lady with the big red truck."

Her husband knelt beside her. Concerned about his wife, yet at the same time uncomfortable about all the attention they had attracted, he stroked her cheek and encouraged her to get up — unless she was hurt. Behind them, still facing away, Frogger stood with his arms around the twins, assuming that he was shielding them from their mother's dying moments. But, in reality, they had other issues on their minds.

"Why did Frogger push Mommy down? Is he mad at her?"

"He didn't push her. She fell."

"Did not."

"Did too."

"Not."

"Too."

Welcome to 'Tichville'

It took Doc Timmerman only 20 minutes to clear the track and bring the fair back to order. Binoculars in his right hand and walkie-talkie in his left, he assumed control of the situation down on the track without even having to leave the grandstand. He called for support from the fire department, relaying a message to Dolly Gilmore to dispatch the department's first-aid vehicle — a 50-year-old Chevy panel van that had once seen service as a military ambulance during the Korean War. Within 15 minutes of his call, Mrs. Troth was strapped onto a backboard, her legs, arms and head immobilized by a confusion of straps and Velcro that had been secured by a half-dozen eager firefighters anxious to put their first-aid training to full use.

Fearful of a lawsuit at the best of times, Doc was more than a little taken aback to see that after 150 years, the racetrack's first Harvest Fair accident victim was the same woman who had threatened to sue the fire department and his

135

son just the day before.

"We're not taking any chances on this one," he barked into his walkie-talkie. "You load her into that rattletrap and get her to the hospital on the double. Better let Randy drive. I need the rest of you back at your posts. Between runaway pigs and a nearsighted jaywalker, we're almost a half-hour behind schedule."

And so, while any other fairground fainting victim would have been given a free Frostee-Freeze and 15 minutes in a lawn chair beneath a shady tree, Sara Troth was whisked to the hospital in Wamble and subjected to a long and exhaustive series of x-rays and tests until 6 o'clock that evening, when doctors finally declared her completely unharmed. The only damage, they would later report with a smile, was to her blue-denim designer outfit, which had been permanently stained when she fell into a fresh cow pie on the track.

As they were loading his wife into the old Chevy van, Mr. Troth looked on fretfully, unsure of what to do. The firefighters were adamant that she be taken to the hospital for observation, but having witnessed the whole thing, he could not believe that Sara had suffered any injury worse than acute embarrassment.

After closing the rear doors of the van, Randy Timmerman asked whether he would like to accompany his wife to the hospital. At first, Dunston Troth had hesitated. If he went along, he would have to bring the twins, as Sara would never forgive him if he left them behind with Frogger Archibald — especially at a place as dangerous as the Harvest Fair. But the prospect of spending the entire afternoon at the hospital with two rambunctious 4-year-olds was equally unappealing.

Finally, he made up his mind and waved his hand in the air.

"Why don't you take her to the hospital and have them get in touch if they find anything serious? In the meantime, I'll stay here with the boys for a bit. They haven't had a chance to go on any of the rides yet."

Randy laughed in agreement. "Yeah. I figure you're right. Just make sure you take her some clean clothes when you pick her up. I noticed she chose a nice soft place to land when she fell, and you'd probably attract a carload of flies if she wore that outfit home."

And then, to add a bit more drama to the day, Randy flipped on the ambulance's flashing lights and moaning siren as he headed down the track.

* * *

Frogger, of course, became something of a hero that day, for if he had not pulled her out of the horse's path when he did, Sara Troth might well have been seriously injured or even killed. Certainly that was Dunston Troth's feeling about the incident, and he gave his young neighbor two crisp $20 bills to show his gratitude.

"Take this," he urged. "Go on all the rides you want, and if you spend it all, come back for some more."

Frogger tried to refuse but was gracious enough to accept the bills after they had been offered twice more. By this time, his parents had joined him, as had dozens of other fairgoers, and everyone was hugging him and slapping him on the back and shoulders, mussing his hair and stroking his pie-covered cheeks. The commotion continued for several minutes, until the steely voice of Doc Timmerman rang out over the public-address system: "Please clear the track. The next race will start in five minutes. Parents are asked to bring their babies to the grandstand for the baby contest. Final judging at the Kitchen 'N Craft Shed starts in 10 minutes. Be sure you have your entries registered. We have a winner to announce in the giant-pumpkin contest . . . "

* * *

It was almost 4 o'clock before Frogger got back over to the pile of shoes for a short visit with Bug and her father. His parents had decided that their son's new status as a local hero warranted a dinner in Amaranth, and he was on his way home to clean up and get changed.

He found Bug and her dad in good spirits, although for very different reasons. As a concession to the warmth of the day, Bug's father had shed his sheepskin vest and had traded his cowboy boots for a mismatched pair of rock-climbing slippers that made him look like an elf on the way to a rock concert. He was in constant motion, elated by the success of their shoe sale. It had proved to be such a success, in fact, that at noon, the site had been officially designated The Shoe Pile by Doc Timmerman. A volunteer with a ladder had erected an official sign on a nearby light standard shortly afterward, and people had swarmed to the site all day. It seemed that Tichburg was crazy about unmatched shoes.

Bug was happy because the day was finally over.

"This is one shoe salesgirl who is looking forward to a hot bath and a short trip to a long salad bar," she announced when Frogger asked how she was doing. It had not been a bad day, she admitted, although there had been one large, obnoxious

138

teenager with greasy hair and a bad complexion who had tried to give her a hard time.

Nicky Knowlton, thought Frogger, shaking his head sympathetically.

"He just sort of hung around pretending to be a sideshow barker, calling people over to look at the alien shoe freaks. He kept it up for about 20 minutes, until the old guy with the white pickup truck drove up and asked him if he wanted a ride. I don't know what that was about, but he sure disappeared in a hurry."

"Yeah, that was my new friend Doc Timmerman," interrupted her father. "He says that there are so many people talking about our little business here, he wants to make sure we come back next year. Sort of make it an annual event."

"So business was good?" asked Frogger.

"Let's just say we sold about 600 shoes today. That's more than I dreamed possible, and Bug will tell you I dream pretty big most of the time."

Bug rolled her eyes.

"Roll those eyes of yours all you want, Bug. This is one lucky place we just landed in. We got our grubstake together in a single day, and that's reason enough for us to stick around for a while."

"In Tichville?" Bug groaned.

"Tichburg. It's called Tichburg," corrected Frogger kindly.

"Why not? The people are friendly, and there's got to be some great places to live around here," he replied.

"You can't be serious," complained Bug. "What are we going to do here?"

"There's plenty to do," said Frogger. "You could go to my

139

school, and I'm sure it'd be easy to find a decent house. Folks are pretty nice, and my dad says all you need is some good ideas and you can succeed anywhere."

"Truer words wuz never spoken."

It was Cigar Davis. "It's why I made my way back here," he continued. "I got tired of all the goings-on I've seen fer the past 15 years. Too many people chasin' the almighty dollar without doin' anyone else a lick o' good. I started out here, 'n by gum, I'm gonna spend my final days here too. It's a fine little village. I fergot just how much I missed it 'til yesterday. Now, you folks'd fit in nicely. Ya did a whole lot of good fer people today."

Looking down at Cigar's feet, Frogger noticed that the old man had also shopped at The Shoe Pile earlier in the day.

"New shoes, Cigar? How do you like them?" he inquired.

"First comfortable ones my feet have seen since the army."

He lifted one foot to show off an ultrawide mauve jogger. On his other foot, he wore a slightly wider black one, and in combination, the shoes gave him the appearance of having webbed feet.

"Yessir, we've done a big business today," announced Bug's father. "And we have you to thank, Frogger. Why don't you help yourself to another pair — on the house."

But, instead, Frogger leaned over and whispered a request in his ear. Bug's dad smiled and nodded his agreement. Then, seeing the Troth twins walking past with their father after having had a few pony rides in the back field, Frogger waved them over and lifted each of them up onto the remaining pile.

"Find something that fits," he told them. "The treat's on

140

Bug's father. Just don't get anything that lets you run too fast. I don't think Tichburg is ready for that."

Mr. Troth was enjoying the company of his new neighbors, smiling eagerly at their jokes as he watched his boys clamber about, waist-deep in shoes.

"Hurry it up in there," he called. "We have to pick up your mother at the hospital soon."

"Say, yer goin' ta Wamble, are ya?" asked Cigar. "I need ta get ta the bank before it closes. Could ya give me a lift? I'd be mighty grateful, 'n we can pick up yer missus on the way back."

* * *

Half an hour later, Frogger was on Mrs. Gilmore's front veranda describing the events of the day to her when the Red Menace drove by, heading up the hill out of Tichburg. Dunston Troth honked the horn as the vehicle roared past, and all four of its occupants waved, including Cigar Davis.

"Now there's an odd sight," observed Mrs. Gilmore, deciding not to complain aloud at the speed of the truck. "My father always said that if you sat out here long enough, you'd eventually see every conceivable thing. I guess he was right."

The Continuing Adventures of
Bug and Frogger

When Frogger recovered Cigar Davis's childhood treasures, the old man managed to avoid telling any of the children what was in the small cigar box and the biscuit tin. (And even Cigar seemed to have forgotten about the ragged scrapbook that was also hidden under the floorboards in the crawl space.)

But Cigar Davis won't be able to keep his secret from Frogger for long, as readers will find out in *Bug*, the next title in the *Adventures of Bug and Frogger Series*. Many of the contents are just keepsakes from Cigar's own childhood in the village of Tichburg, but a few of them will change the lives of their owner and his friends.

The population of Tichburg is also increasing by two residents, with the arrival of 12-year-old Bug Hapensak and her wild father, Walter, who is convinced that life in a small country village is just what Bug needs — even though the village might not be ready for either of them.

The Author and the Illustrator

Frank B. Edwards and his wife Susan spent 16 years living in a small, friendly village that was very much like Tichburg. Their 150-year-old house overlooked a tumbledown dam that served as the village swimming hole, and they spent many summer nights together on their front porch listening to the water rush over the falls.

A former magazine editor and feature writer, Frank started writing children's books in 1990 and has more than 20 to his credit. He and Susan, a teacher, have three children, a grandchild and an ancient white cat.

Illustrator *John Bianchi* is also a children's author and has worked with Frank since their magazine careers crossed paths in 1980. Since 1986, they have created almost 40 children's books together, even though they now live 3,000 miles apart. One of John's best-known books is *Snowed in at Pokeweed Public School.*

You can contact John and Frank at: authors@Pokeweed.com

144